SIXTH-GRADE

glommers, **norks,** and me

SIXTH-GRADE

glommers, **norks,** and me

Lisa Papademetriou

SCHOLASTIC INC.

New York Toronto London Auckland
Sydney Mexico City New Delhi Hong Kong

ISBN 978-0-545-24222-6

12 11 10 9 8 7 6 5 4 3   10 11 12 13 14 15/0

Printed in the U.S.A.   40

First Scholastic printing, March 2010

Lexile is a registered trademark of MetaMetrics, Inc.

This book is for *Helen Perelman,*
who Makes Things Happen,
with special thanks to *Elizabeth Rudnick,*
Queen of the LFC.

stealth freak•ies \ 'stelth 'free-keez\ *n* : a feeling that comes before dread, i.e., when you just feel a little bit sick, before you realize that anything is wrong, or that your whole life is about to change for the worse, or something else equally bad

"You aren't taking this seriously, Allie," said my best friend in the world, Tamara Thompson. "This is the kind of thing that can make or break your whole year." She crossed her arms over her chest, frowning at me from her seat in my desk chair.

It was actually kind of funny to see her sitting there in the chair that I hardly ever use. I mean, I use the chair—but only to throw clothes on. Of course, that might have to change soon, I thought as I looked at my messy desk. It was covered in glitter and a few half-ripped-off photos from magazines I had accidentally glued to the top while making a collage last year. There was a pair of dirty socks sitting next to the stapler, and a withered old apple core that must have been about as old as I was hanging out by a dust-covered cube of Post-its. Glick.

Tam picked an ancient plastic toy horse off my desk, turned it over in her fingers, and set it down again. I had developed an obsession with ponies in first grade, and immediately started collecting toy horses and begging my mom for a pony for Christmas. But Mom said no way. Instead I got a soccer ball. That was why my walls were covered in soccer posters and the collages I had made of Mia Hamm and David Beckham. My bookshelves were crowded with ribbons and trophies from tournaments. Plus, I'd won MVP three years in a row.

It's weird how—when you have stuff long enough—you just stop seeing it. All of that junk had been there for years, but suddenly, I was embarrassed by my plastic horses, my messy desk, and my even messier room. I can't start sixth grade this way, I decided, mentally vowing to clean the place up that night.

"School starts tomorrow," Tam went on, as though we hadn't spent the past three months talking about how nervous and excited we were about middle school. See, Tam and I were headed to a "magnet" school for the so-called "smart" kids. I'm not really sure how that happened, but Tam claims it had to do with some test we took in the second grade. Personally, I think it probably had more to do with my dad calling the school board and threatening to unleash holy heck if I didn't get into the program, but whatever. The point is: almost all of the other kids we knew were headed to Twin Pines Middle School, while we were headed to Grover Cleveland. "So what are you going to wear?" Tam asked seriously.

"I don't know," I told her. "Jeans?"

Tam gave her curly black hair a toss and let out a frustrated "Grr." Tam is my best friend, but we're way different. She's always been the prettiest girl in the class, and she always dresses really well—she's just good at that kind of stuff. Like right now, for example. It was a summer Sunday, and she had on a bright blue tank and a tan skort, both of which looked brand-new. If I'd put on that outfit, I would have gotten a stain on the front within five minutes.

"*I'm* going to wear a skirt," Tam said, twirling in the desk chair.

"I don't even own a skirt," I told her. "None that fit, anyway."

"What about the khaki one?" Tam suggested.

Wow. Tam was right. I *did* have a khaki skirt . . . somewhere. My stepmom, Marci, had given it to me—proving beyond a reasonable doubt that she doesn't know me at all. I'd worn it once, like, two months before. Feeling kind of impressed that Tam knew my clothes better than I did, I walked to my closet and flipped through the hangers. "Not here." My eyes moved to my bed. I had a dim memory of kicking it under there after Sally Chin's birthday/Fourth of July party.

Catching my look, Tam slid off the desk chair and peered under the bed. "Oh my God," she said, as if I had a dead body under there. I mean— what's the big deal? I thought. Hasn't she ever seen a hidden mountain of junk before? In case it isn't blatantly clear, I'm not exactly into cleaning, and neither is my mom. There was so much fossilized crud under that bed, I could have turned it into a natural history museum exhibit.

Tam pulled out a plastic mug filled with

bluish mold. "Allison Louise Kimball, what is this?" she asked, doing a really killer imitation of my dad.

I flushed a little. "Um . . . milk?" I guessed, although the stuff in the mug wasn't even liquid anymore.

Tam jumped away from the mug, which clunked on the floor. "Gross!" Still, I guess the mass of junk was kind of fascinating, or something, because she put her hand under the bed again and fished out a pair of sunglasses wrapped in a giant lint ball.

"I've been looking for those!" I said, grabbing the glasses. Oh, glick. The linty junk was kind of greasy. Actually, Tam was right—this was really gross.

"What's this?" Tam asked. I winced as she scraped an ancient, dust-covered notebook across the dirty floor under my bed. Tam blew some of the dust off the cover. "LFC," she read aloud. "Allie," Tam said with a grin, "do you know what this is?"

I cringed as she flipped it open to the first page. "Living proof that we used to be major dorks?" The LFC Club had been Tam's idea. LFC stood for Look for Clues, and it was supposed to be like the Baby-sitters Club, only without the babysitting. Once a week, the members would meet by the swings at recess to discuss the "clues" we had been looking for—evidence that the guys we were crushing on liked us back. There were only three of us in the club, so the reporting never took very long. It was kind of like being a very lame spy.

"'October fourteenth. Chris G. asked Allie if he could use her pen,'" Tamara read aloud.

I snorted. Chris Gibson was a guy a grade above us who I used to have this mad crush on. One day, while we were at recess, he asked me if he could borrow a pen. I said, "Sure," but when I reached for my backpack—I don't know, I picked it up by the side, or something. Anyway, everything spilled out into this big patch of dirt, and Chris was, like, "Never mind," and that was the last time I ever talked to him.

Anyway, the fact that Chris asked me for a pen was considered by the club to be a major clue that he was into me. Just to show how very far into la-la land we were, I will tell you that it was recorded in the notebook in *red* pen, with hearts around it.

Smiling, Tam continued to flip through the notebook. "'Heather J. is a complete snig, and keeps squeeling whenever Brian B. makes his rat face,'" Tam read aloud. "'She totally likes him.'" There was a star by the word *snig*, and then a definition: "snobby pig who likes to squeel."

"Please destroy it," I begged. "I don't want anyone to know that I couldn't spell *squeal*."

Tam giggled. "I'd forgotten that you were nuts about vocabulary words back then."

Actually, I'd been making up words ever since Ms. Ratner's third-grade class. She always made us look up words in the dictionary when we didn't know the meaning. And that was when I realized that sometimes you needed just the opposite—you had a meaning, but there wasn't a word to fit it. So I started making up my own vocabulary. The truth is, I still do it.

Tam kept reading. "'Renee and Tam think—'"

"Alli-i-ie!" My older brother, Lionel, has this annoying way of shouting my name that makes it sound like something heavy has fallen on his foot. It gets on my nerves.

"What?" I screamed.

My door popped open, and Lionel stuck his raggedy head inside. His hair is the same color as mine—dark red—but his is straight instead of curly. His eyebrows flew up when he saw Tam. Lionel has always said that Tam was way too cool to be my best friend. "Hey, Tam."

"Hi, Lionel."

"Greetings, Prime Minister of Jerkistan," I put in. "What do you want?"

Lionel's eyes clouded over as he glanced at me. "I want you to stop touching my stuff." Lionel is two years older, and I was *not* happy that we were about to be in the same school again, starting tomorrow. "Where's my iPod?"

"How should I know?" I gave my hair a toss and leaned back on my elbows.

Lionel gritted his teeth. "Because you took it."

"No, I didn't."

"Then where is it?" Lionel's face was starting to turn red, a sure sign that he was getting mad.

"Maybe it's in your pigsty of a room," I said. "Look under your trough." I just said that to bug him. The truth is, Lionel is way neater than me. I mean, he organizes his socks by *color*. His CDs are alphabetized. He reads his comic books once, then seals them in plastic bags. I'm telling you, he's sick.

Lionel gave this little lunge toward me, and I screeched, "Mom!" which normally would have been completely pointless—Mom likes to let us "work out our own differences"—but she happened to be walking down the hall at that very minute.

"What's going on?" Mom demanded, poking her red head into my room. She has the most beautiful hair. It's really red—not brownish, like Lionel's and mine—and it falls in even waves instead of rising in a ball of frizz. "Oh, hi, Tam. I didn't realize you were over." Mom smiled, her gray eyes crinkling at the edges.

"Hi, Ms. Fine." Tam is superpolite around grown-ups.

You're probably wondering why Mom and I have different last names. It's because Mom went back to her maiden name after my parents got divorced. In a way, it's kind of weird to have the same name as my dad, who lives in another state, instead of Mom, who I see every day. But I didn't get to choose my last name when they split up, and I knew that Dad would freak if I changed it now, so I just stuck with Kimball.

"Lionel, you left your iPod in the back pocket of your jeans," Mom said, holding it out. "I found it in the laundry."

Lionel took it, his face burning. I gave him a smug little smile as Mom held out the phone to me. "Dad wants to talk to you."

I took the phone and retreated to my desk while Lionel showed Tam his iPod. Mom dug around in my closet for my laundry.

"Dad?" I said into the receiver.

"Hi, sweetheart." Dad's voice is a warm rumble. When I was little, I used to love it when he read stories to me. My dad is huge, and I would cuddle next to him before he tucked me in. I didn't even really care which story he chose—just hearing his deep growly voice made me feel safe. "I wanted to say, good luck tomorrow."

"Thanks. I guess I'm a little nervous."

"Don't be," Dad said. "Just give them your best smile." This is typical Dad advice. He used to be a marine, and isn't afraid of much. "Do you have a pretty dress?"

I sighed. I love my dad, but he always acts like I'm about four years old. I guess it's because I *was* four when he moved to Ohio. "I think I'm just going to wear jeans."

"Jeans?" I could hear the frown in his voice.

"Well," I hedged, "maybe my white pants." I should have known. Dad is the only person in the world who cares about how I dress even more than Tam does.

"Pants? Don't you think you should get a little dressed up for the first day of school?" I knew he was thinking of the skirt Marci had given me.

"My white pants are dressy," I said.

Dad sighed. "Okay. Well, have a good first day. I want a full report. Would you put your mother back on the phone?"

"Okay," I told him. "Bye, Dad."

"Yes?" Mom said, cradling the phone between

her ear and her shoulder as she scooped up my laundry—which had somehow landed all around my basket instead of in it. "Howard, I think pants are fine." There was a pause, then Mom said, "I think she should wear what she wants." She blew her bangs out of her face, and rubbed her neck the way she does when she's feeling stressed. Phone conversations with my dad usually have that effect on her. "Lionel's here, would you like to speak to him?"

Lionel bounded off the bed and grabbed the cordless. "Hey, Dad!" he chirped. He and Dad get along great. They're on the same wavelength, somehow. Mom picked up the laundry basket and followed Lionel out the door.

"So, what did your dad think you should wear?" Tam wanted to know.

"A dress," I told her. "But he's a dad—he doesn't know anything."

Tam nodded. "Allie," she said slowly, "what if everyone at Grover Cleveland is mad cool, and I look like a nork?"

I actually laughed at that. "Look—Lionel goes there, and he's a major nerd. Besides, you can always hang with me."

"But we only have one class together," Tam pointed out.

I sighed. That part was true. "Well, there's before school, and after. And we have the same lunch." I picked up the dusty old LFC notebook. "Look, if we could stay friends through this," I said, holding up the notebook, "we'll stay friends through sixth grade."

"Best friends," Tam corrected. She held out her hand. On the index finger of her right hand was a slim blue enamel band that we had bought together over the summer.

I put my hand over hers, showing her that I was wearing my friendship ring, too. "Yeah, best friends."

Tam took the notebook and flipped through it again. "You know, you should keep another notebook this year. A record of middle school."

Actually, that wasn't such a bad idea. I had high hopes for sixth grade. Everyone warned me that it was much harder than elementary school, but it also seemed like more fun. More grown-up, or something. "Okay," I said, pulling out one of the clean new notebooks that Mom had bought for me. It had soccer balls on the front and crackled as I opened it.

"A soccer notebook?" Tam asked, smiling a little.

Hmm, I thought, looking down at the cover, is it babyish? "Are you saying that you think the soccer notebook is lamer than the pink-with-red-hearts LFC notebook?" I asked.

"Good point," Tam admitted. I slipped a pen with blue sparkly ink out of the cup on my desk and sat on the bed beside her.

One day till sixth grade, and Tam is afraid of looking like a nork, I wrote. My handwriting hadn't gotten much better than it was in the third grade, I'm sorry to say.

"Better explain what a nork is," Tam said, pointing to the page.

I nodded and wrote in the definition.

———◆———

nork \'nork\ *n* : someone beyond both nerditude and dorkdom; a dweeb squared.

But that's not going to happen, I added to the notebook. *Allie is going to wear white pants, as her khaki skirt has disappeared into the Bermuda*

Rectangle known as her room. Then I flipped it closed, picked up the heinous, dust-covered LFC notebook, and placed them both side by side on the shelf. I turned to Tam and smiled.

She smiled back, but for some reason, the stealth freakies crawled down my spine.

It's just nerves, I told myself. This year is going to be great.

After all, I had my best friend. What else did I need?

- 2 -

blarg \'blarg\ **1:** *v* to insult rudely and loudly, to diss
beyond normal diss-dom **2:** *n* an insult that leaves you
feeling like the biggest nork that ever walked the face
of the planet

"Take three steps back and don't tell anyone
you're my sister," Lionel said the minute we
arrived at the bus stop.

"Why?" I demanded, hitching my nearly
empty book bag higher onto my shoulder.
"Because you're too cool to be seen with me?"

"No—because you look like Strawberry
Shortcake." Lionel smiled smugly.

I looked down at my outfit in horror. I was
wearing my white pants and a pink T-shirt.
Ohmygosh, I thought, wondering what I had been
thinking when I got dressed that morning. You
can't just go around wearing pink and white when
you have a curly mop of red hair and freckles.
People mock you.

But it was too late now, and stupid Lionel

knew it. That was why he had been so quiet at the breakfast table. He didn't want to blarg my outfit in time for me to change.

Did I mention that my brother is an evil genius?

Thankfully, Tamara walked up to the bus stop at that very moment.

"Tell me that I don't look like Strawberry Shortcake," I begged.

Looking my outfit up and down, Tam gave me this sort of *Gee I'm really sorry* wince, and said, "Lots of people *like* shortcake."

Lionel laughed from his place three paces away, and I sighed. That's the thing about Tam— she never lies to save your feelings. Sometimes I wish she would.

The bus pulled up with a rattling shudder and the doors sighed open. I stepped aboard and looked around, thinking, Who are all of these people?

I knew that Grover Cleveland Middle School was huge—I'd seen it when Mom and I had to drop off Lionel for chess club—and I knew that kids from lots of different elementary schools went there. But somehow, I wasn't ready for a busload of strangers.

Lionel headed toward the back where his best friends—Jed and Sammy, the Nerdtastic Duo—were saving him a seat.

Tam found us seats in the center as the doors closed and the bus started to pull away.

Just then, a voice shouted, "Hold up! Hold up! Sto-o-o-o-op!" Someone banged on the side of the bus, and we jerked to a stop. The doors hissed open, and my friend Justin Thyme (I swear that's his name—Justin's dad is a huge joker) scrambled aboard. Breathing hard, Justin flashed the bus driver a huge grin and said, "Okay, you can go now."

The bus driver glared as the bus doors slapped closed. Justin flailed a little as the bus lurched forward, then recovered and started down the aisle.

"As usual, you're Justin Thyme," I told him as he took the seat in front of mine. My standard joke. Everyone's standard joke. With a name like that, you'd think he could try to be punctual once or twice in his life. "Nice entrance, by the way."

"I like to make an impression," Justin joked, flipping his hair like some Hollywood starlet.

"Hey, Justin," Tam said from her seat across from mine.

"Oh, hey, Tam," Justin said. He looked down at his backpack quickly, and moved it from the seat to the floor. Then he moved it up again. He opened his mouth like he was about to say something, but nothing came out. He just smiled at me.

Okay, that was slightly weird. Justin is usually really funny and fun to hang with. He lives two doors down, and we play soccer sometimes. But guys (including Justin, I guess) tend to get shy around Tam. Have I mentioned that she's really pretty? Sometimes, it can be kind of annoying.

I looked at her. She was wearing this cute yellow tank and a blue-and-yellow-flowered flippy skirt. Her long black hair curled around her face, and her dark eyes looked bigger than usual. I realized suddenly that she was wearing makeup.

I felt like an even bigger nork than I had before.

Why didn't I let Tam choose an outfit for me yesterday? I wondered.

The bus shuddered to a stop and we picked up three enormous eighth graders and a kid with frizzy brown hair, who looked like he was probably in sixth. The eighters bounded to the back, while the frizzy-haired kid looked around, then sat down in the front row.

You know how you can sometimes spot the class nerd a mile off? I had no doubts—this was the guy. It wasn't like he looked like a total weirdo, or anything—no Star Trek T-shirt, no Coke bottle glasses, no headgear. But his shirt was this really ugly shade of puce. And his leather shoes were the lace-up kind . . . and I could tell he was wearing them with sweat socks. Plus, he had a Snoopy pin on his backpack.

My outfit was a tragic mistake, but this guy's clothes were Nork City, USA.

A loud burst of laughter came from the back of the bus, and I turned around to see Lionel high-fiving one of the huge eighth graders. I frowned.

Since when is my brother cool? I wondered. I mean, he's a nork. Isn't he? I thought. But I was starting to realize that he had sort of "cooled it down" since hitting middle school. His clothes, for example. Untucked plaid over too-large khakis. They blended right in. And his hair was shaggy in the way that all of the guys' hair seemed to be shaggy. Middle-school camouflage.

I turned back toward the frizzy-haired kid again. What did my brother know that this kid didn't?

With another rumble and growl, the bus pulled up to the front of the school, which was even bigger and more prisonlike than I remembered. I had to stifle the groan as I looked out the smeary bus window. Everyone was dressed up for the first day of school. All of the kids looked older, and half of them had clearly had their clothes shipped to them from MTV. Everyone was clustered in groups, and each little pack seemed to have its own dress code. Some of the groups were familiar. For example, the mathletes, with their enormous backpacks, were standing on the concrete front steps. The student government types, in their preppy, well-ironed khakis, were standing near the big tree on the front lawn. And the tough kids—ripped jeans, concert T-shirts, messy hair—were over in the far corner. But there were other groups at Grover Cleveland, ones I didn't know. I felt like I had entered some kind of wildlife special. You know, one of the ones in which the innocent seal gets eaten by a grizzly bear.

Perfect, I thought. Frizzy-Haired Kid and I will fit right in. We'll be the seals.

"How many classes do we have together, again?" Tam whispered nervously as she eyed the school.

"One," I said miserably.

"I guess it's time to start the first day of the rest of our middle-school life," Justin said as he slid into the aisle.

Yeah, I thought as I stood up. Time to join the other wild creatures of the sixth grade.

---

glom•mers \'glom-ers\ *n* : **1:** girls who cling to each other in groups **2:** friends who never go anywhere without each other, like they're tied together with invisible string

Tam and I had to split up to find our lockers and

homerooms. Then I sat through English, Spanish, and math in kind of a daze. Mostly we played "getting to know you" games, collected our books, and wrote down lists of supplies we'd need for the class while the teacher made a permanent seating chart. It was strange—I'd never had to play a "getting to know you" game in class before. In elementary school, I'd always known everyone. They were just the kids from the neighborhood— the same kids I'd been going to school with since kindergarten. But here, I couldn't remember a single person's name.

Well, except for Orren Kendall, aka Frizzy-Haired Kid. Since my last name is Kimball, so far I was seated next to Orren in every single class. I bet people thought we were swapping fashion tips.

When the bell for fourth period rang, I breathed a sigh of relief. Finally, science. My class with Tam. I pressed my books to my chest and kept my head down as I headed down the hall. I didn't have anyone to walk with during the passing periods, and it was embarrassing—especially since I kept getting lost and wandering around with this totally fake *I swear I know where I'm going and besides I have friends they're just not in this class* look on my face. But that was about to change—for one period, at least.

But when I walked into science, Tam was already seated at a lab table with someone else— a girl with long blond hair. It took me a moment to realize who it was . . . and then the world seemed to tilt on its axis.

Renee Anderson.

I caught my breath. Oh, no, I thought. Nonononononononono. My heart pounded in my ears.

"Allie!" Tam cried, waving me over.

Why is Tam sitting with her? I wondered frantically. My head felt like it was wobbling, balloonlike, on top of my neck as I walked toward their lab table.

"Allie, look who's here!" Tam cried, as though it was perfectly normal that she was seated with the person who had been her own archenemy for three years. "Renee is in five of my classes!"

"Oh," I said, trying to smile. "That's . . . that's great."

"Hello, Allie," Renee said.

Ugh. Even the way she said *hello* instead of *hi* made me want to barf.

Okay, I should back up. Renee used to be our friend. In fact, she used to be the LFC's third member . . . until things blew up. I'll admit, it was partially my fault. It was my stupid idea that we start a slam book. I thought that— since there were only three of us—we would all just write nice things about each other, and then we'd feel great and everybody would be happy. But under Tamara's "face" section, Renee wrote "kind of flat." I didn't think it was such a big deal, but Tam was *furious*. She stopped talking to Renee, and I didn't want to stop hanging with Tam . . . so I stopped talking to Renee, too. Then Renee became best friends with Hallie McDermott, and the two of them became glommers. They just latched on to each other, and then the two of them went everywhere together, like Tweedledum and Tweedledee, and that was the end of that.

Over the years, it had somehow morphed

into this "We hate Renee" thing. And then Renee had a different teacher for fifth grade, so we never really saw her much.

"Pull up a chair," Tam told me now.

All *three* of us are going to be lab partners? I thought. Oh, glick—where's Hallie when you need her? But Tam didn't seem to be kidding, so I grabbed a chair, which let out a wild squeak as I dragged it across the floor.

"Um, excuse me," said the teacher from the front of the room. She was tall and thin, with sparse brown hair and too much blue eye shadow over pale blue eyes. If the chalkboard was to be trusted, her name was Mrs. Larsen.

I pointed to myself. "Me?"

"Yes. Please don't move the chairs." She fixed me with that strange ice-blue stare.

"We just wanted to have three at this table . . ." I started.

"Two at a table," Mrs. Larsen said. "There's an empty seat at the back."

Her tone sounded final, so I turned to Renee. She knew that Tam and I were best friends. She had to move.

"See you after class," Renee told me, flipping her blond hair over her shoulder.

My heart fluttered like a frantic butterfly. This was my only class with Tam—and I wasn't even going to get to sit with her? I stared at Tam, who shrugged helplessly and glanced at the teacher, who was still giving me the blue–eye shadow glare.

That was it. I didn't have a choice. I made my way to the back of the class.

Oh, no. I had to take a deep breath to keep myself from groaning. Naturally, the only seat open was the one next to Orren Kendall.

He didn't even look up as I plopped into the chair next to his.

Great.

———◦◦———

stink•prise \\'stink-priz\\ *n* : something unexpected and unwanted, like a pair of dirty underwear in your Christmas stocking

Why didn't you save me a seat in science? The question had been ringing in my ears all day. But I hadn't asked it. Not yet. I just couldn't—it freaked me out too much. Did it mean that Tam was mad at me, or something? But that didn't make sense. So then, what? The whole thing made me so crazy that I just kept quiet.

Besides, even if I had dared to ask, I hadn't had a chance. Renee sat with me and Tam during lunch. And after school, the minute Tam and I sat down on the school bus, Justin—who seemed to have gotten over his shyness—started chattering up a storm. So I had to wait until we got off for any privacy. Justin waved and walked toward his house with Jim Donelly, and Lionel sprinted way ahead of us. By the time I had a chance to talk to Tam in private, I really didn't know how to bring it up.

"So," I said brightly as we fell into step next to each other, "did you hear that announcement they made in homeroom? First soccer practice tomorrow." Tam and I had been on a league team together the year before. "We should join. Then we can hang on the team, and go to the big sports banquet at the end of the term." The Cleveland sports banquet was held twice a year, and I guess it was a huge deal. Everyone who played a sport got to go.

"Yeah . . ." Tam's voice sounded kind of . . . wispy. Like a thin strip of cloud across a bright blue sky.

"You want to meet me before?" I asked. "We can warm up together."

Tam squinted as she looked into the distance. "I was thinking of maybe . . . going out for cheer squad."

"Cheer squad?" I stopped in my tracks.

"Yeah." Tam looked apologetic. "I mean, soccer is your thing, Allie. I've never been very good."

"That's not true!" I said, even though it was true. Tam had actually kicked the ball into the wrong goal during one game. It kind of worked out, though, because the other team started laughing so hard that we managed to score on them. "You won't even know anyone on cheer squad," I pointed out, my heart fluttering.

"Well . . . Renee is going to try out, too."

"Is Hallie trying out?" I asked. I know, that was kind of mean. But I was feeling kind of mean. Having Renee in my life again was kind of a stinkprise.

"Hallie's going to Twin Pines," Tam said.

Twin Pines Middle School. That figured. That was where almost everyone we know was going.

"Allie," Tam went on quickly, "I just wanted to tell you that I'm so sorry about science. The thing is, when Renee told me that Hallie was going to Twin Pines, I felt kind of bad for her. And Renee doesn't know anyone at Cleveland, either, so we got to talking in homeroom, and . . . It's just—we walked together from Spanish class, and when I got into science, I didn't see you. . . . So Renee and I sat together. I really thought we'd be able to have three to a table. . . ." Tam's voice trailed off when she saw my glazed expresson.

I nodded, even though *I* would have saved the seat. I wouldn't have made her sit with a norky lab partner. But Tam really did look sorry, and I have to admit that I was kind of relieved. So she wasn't mad at me. She had just made a mistake. Anyone can make a mistake.

"Look, don't be upset about soccer," Tam said, taking my hand. Her blue friendship ring pressed against my fingers. "We'll still get to hang, and we'll still go to the banquet together, okay? Cheer squad goes, too."

"Okay," I said. But I couldn't help feeling that it just wouldn't be the same.

jock•iss•i•ma \jok-'iss-i-ma\ *n* : an excellent female
athlete

I sat on the bench, pulling on my cleats and
trying not to be utterly obvious as I looked
around, sizing up the other players. The Cleveland
team—the Tigers—had a reputation as total
jockissimas.

A tall girl with a long brown ponytail and
hazel eyes loped down the field. She was slim
and superfast, like one of those greyhound racing
dogs. With a whiplash move, she cut left, then
slammed the ball into the net. Holy guacamole, I
thought.

"Jack!" A girl with a wide smile waved to the
tall girl and trotted out onto the field.

Jack? I thought. What kind of name is that for
a girl?

"Hey, Elena!" Jack shouted.

I hadn't seen either of these girls in any of my
classes, so I figured that they were older—seventh

or eighth grade. Another group of about ten girls was running a kicking drill at the other goal. I figured anyone brave enough to hang out on the field must be a returning team member. Everyone else was warming up on the sidelines.

Jack and Elena squared off, with Jack trying to get the ball to the goal. Even with her lightning-fast moves, she wasn't having much luck against Elena. Jack cut left, then right, but Elena dogged her every step. Finally, Elena managed to steal the ball. She grinned at her own cool move.

I couldn't help smiling, too. Elena had coarse brown hair that hung around her round face in scraggly waves and dancing black eyes.

"Not bad for a sweeper," Jack said, clapping Elena on the shoulder.

Oh, no, I thought, groaning mentally. Sweeper was my position.

Even though I knew the Tigers were a great team, I'd been secretly hoping that I would get to start this year. I get antsy just sitting around on the bench—I always want to play. But I'd definitely be second string to Elena.

But there wasn't enough time to feel really sorry for myself, because just then the coach came out and blew her whistle.

I finished tying up my cleats and trotted over to where the coach was standing. She was short and powerfully built, with dark brown skin and warm brown eyes. Her hair was streaked with gray, but other than that, she looked really young.

"Okay, everyone!" the coach called as the team straggled over. "My name is Andrea Connors. Some of you know me from seventh-grade earth science, and some of you know me from last year, and some of you don't know me at all. So I'm going to pass this around." She held up a clipboard. "Everyone, please write down your name, your favorite position, your e-mail address if you have one, and your phone number."

I looked around. There had to be at least thirty girls standing around. In a way, that was good, because we had enough people to practice against each other with a full team on each side. But in a way, it was bad, because I had a feeling I'd be doing a lot of benchwarming.

"Not everyone will get to start in a game," Coach Connors went on, "but everyone will get to play." The clipboard came around, and I wrote down my information. I hesitated a minute over the favorite position category. But I knew I'd have tough competition no matter what position I chose, so I just scribbled "sweeper" and passed the clipboard to the next girl.

The coach ran through the usual coach speech about how we were going to work hard and have a great year, and blah-blahdy-blah. I was trying to listen to what she was saying, but I couldn't concentrate—I was too eager to get out on the field. The grass was fresh and green from a summer without trampling, and the sun was hot. Finally, Coach wrapped up. Someone handed the clipboard back to her. "Sarah Simmons, take goalie, blue team," Coach announced. She looked up at the short-haired African American girl who stepped forward, smiling shyly. "Welcome back, Sarah," Coach said. "Jacqueline Wallace: right wing, blue team. Good to see you, Jack." The greyhound-like girl went to stand with Sarah. "Sally Chin," Coach said, and I craned my neck to see. I knew Sally! I hadn't seen her since early July, and I hadn't noticed her because she looked different—her hair was braided in cool cornrows and she was tan. But it was her. We weren't best buds, or anything, but at least she was a familiar face.

"Sally," the coach said, "take left wing, blue. Allie Kimball: striker, blue team."

Striker? Oh, great. My stomach felt like it was full of greasy caterpillars. I hate playing any of those scoring positions, but striker is the worst. "Uh, Coach Connors?" I said, raising my hand. "I think there's a mistake. I wrote down *sweeper*."

"You're striker today," Coach said without looking up. "Kristin Dallman, you're sweeper, blue."

I sighed and trudged over to join my teammates as Coach ran through the rest of the positions. Sure enough, Elena was the sweeper for the red team.

"Everyone, take two laps, then head out onto the field," Coach announced.

I settled into a jog, dreading taking the field. Just what I didn't want—to be second or third string in a position I hated. I was actually starting to wish that I had gone out for cheer squad, which is kind of hilarious, given that I had totally twisted my ankle the last time I attempted a cartwheel.

Actually, there had been about five minutes earlier in the day when I truly considered joining the cheer squad. Renee and Tam and I had eaten lunch together out on the patio, and they were talking about the cheers they were going to do for the tryouts, which weren't until the following week. Tam had made up her own cheer, the start of which went something like, "Tigers growl and Tigers bite! Let's go, Tigers! Fight, fight, fight!"

"You may not want to say, 'Tigers bite,'" Renee pointed out. She took a delicate sip of her soda.

Tam looked horrified. "Oh, no! I didn't even think of that."

"Hmm . . ." I said, biting into the fudge brownie my mom had packed into my lunch. "What about 'Tigers growl and Tigers roar! They'll use you to mop the floor!'"

"That's good," Renee told me. She seemed

kind of surprised. "Tam, use that. Why aren't you trying out for the cheer squad, Allie?"

I shrugged. "Because I don't want to break my neck."

"Seriously?" Renee asked. "But you're so coordinated. You're great at sports, right?"

"Yeah," Tam agreed, grabbing my hand. "Come with us, Allie."

I felt this warm glow in the pit of my stomach, like I had just drunk a huge cup of hot chocolate. Renee isn't so bad now, I thought. Actually, she was kind of cool. And I guess I felt flattered that she and Tam thought I'd make a good cheerleader. I even pictured myself with the pom-poms and everything. But cheerleading . . . well, you have to wear a skirt. Besides, Renee was only half right. I'm coordinated—on the soccer field. But cartwheels and roundoffs and junk like that— forget it. "I think I'll stick with soccer," I said finally.

Tam looked disappointed, but not surprised. She knows I'm a soccer girl.

"Oh, well. Less competition for us, right Tam?" Renee had said. And that was that.

I felt someone tap me on the shoulder, snapping me back to the present. "Hey!" Sally said, giving me a brilliant grin.

"Hey, Sally!" Our footfalls fell into the same rhythm as we headed into the last curve of the second lap. "I didn't know you went here."

Sally rolled her eyes. "Please. This place is so huge, your best friend could go here and you'd never know it!"

"Tell me about it," I agreed, feeling silent relief that at least I had lunch and science with Tam.

Once we were finished with our laps, we scrambled to our places. The ball was kicked off, and it immediately headed our way.

Instinctively, I trotted back to protect our goal. A skinny girl with long blond hair was streaking toward Sarah, the goalie. I cut in front of Skinny and managed to steal. Looking around for someone to pass to, I spotted Jack, and kicked the ball her way. She tore down the field, and I trotted after her. It took me a minute to register that I was the striker—I was supposed to be at the other end of the field! I raced toward the red goal just in time for Jack to pass the ball back to me. I had a perfect shot—wide open. My heart nearly exploded out of my chest. Don't screw this up! I thought as I took the shot.

And missed.

I *missed*! Someone dig a hole for me to hide in, I thought as I stared at the ball. This is why I'm a sweeper.

"Kimball!" Coach shouted from the sidelines. "Move it!"

That was when I realized that I had stopped dead in my tracks, while the game had kept going. Elena had the ball, and she was driving it toward the center of the field. I took off after her.

Elena dodged downfield, past two girls trying to defend her. She slammed the ball toward her team's right wing—not in time. Sally intercepted and passed the ball to me.

Oh, God, why does everyone keep passing to me? I thought desperately. I just wanted to get rid of it, so I took the open shot to Jack. She headed it into the goal.

Score!

"Dallman, Kimball, Boynton, Kirikalis, Wallace,

take a rest!" Coach Connors called from the sidelines. "Jackson, Smythe, Laird, Khan, Anderson, sub in!"

That was it. My turn was over. I had to go sit on the sidelines.

Fighting the urge to run up to Coach Connors and tell her that I was a much better player than it seemed, I jogged to the sidelines and flopped on the grass.

"Hey," Elena said, flopping next to me. "What's your name?"

I looked behind me, but there wasn't anyone there. "Allie," I said.

"I'm Elena Kirikalis." The girl leaned back on her elbows and flexed her feet. "It's always rough to come back after the summer. I know I'm going to hurt tomorrow."

"Yeah," I agreed, feeling kind of shy. In a way, sitting with a seventh grader made me feel like less of a nork. And in a way it made the norkitude worse. "Were you on the team last year?"

"Yeah."

"And she has Connors for life science, too," Jack added, trotting up on the tail end of our conversation. "Which means she'll need earplugs for the rest of the year."

Elena grinned. "I love Connors," she said. "Even if she yells a lot."

Jack rolled her eyes. "I hear Connors is the toughest science teacher in the school. I'm hoping that I get Rawlings next year." Then she smiled at me. "Hi, I'm Jack."

"Allie." I adjusted my weight on the soft grass below me. "Wait—you're in sixth?" I asked Jack. "How do you guys know each other?"

"League team," Elena said with a smile.

"That was a nice steal you made, by the way," Jack said, turning to me.

I rolled my eyes. "Nice goal, too," I said sarcastically.

Elena shrugged. "We're all rusty."

I gave her a weak smile. It was a nice thing for her to say, even though she and Jack didn't look too rusty to me.

"Ladies," Coach Connors shouted at us. "Less chatting, more watching. You can learn from your teammates."

I sighed and turned back to face the game.

Yeah, I thought as I watched the girls darting across the field, I have a lot to learn.

———◆———

ac•ci•diss \\'aks-e-diss\ *n* : an accidental insult, the kind that slips out when you have something else on your mind

"Hey, Allie," Justin said as I slipped into the seat across from him. There was only one bus in the afternoon for kids who played sports, and it wasn't as nice as the morning bus. Fossilized gum was stuck between the ridges of the antislide rubber lining the aisle, and the backs of the seats were lined with graffiti. "Where's Tam?"

"Cheer squad hasn't started yet, so I'm riding solo."

"Thanks a lot," Justin said.

I winced at my accidiss. "Sorry—you know what I mean."

"So how'd it go?" he asked.

"Horror movie," I told him. "You?"

"More like a screwball comedy. Some of the guys are having a little trouble working together. But I think I did okay. What happened to you?"

"The coach put me in as the striker. The rest

of the team is really great, and I looked spaztastic."

Justin nodded gravely. He knows how I feel about scoring. Way too much pressure. "There were a couple of really good guys on my team, too—Stuart Jackson and Chris Gibson. Remember Chris? They made the rest of us look pretty bad. But you still have to have eleven on a team, so I think . . ."

This was where I tuned out. Chris Gibson. Of course I remembered him. He was the guy I'd crushed on for all of third and fourth grade. The guy from the LFC. The thought of his blue eyes made my heart give a little stutter. So he was here. At Cleveland. I'd forgotten that he and Justin used to be friends.

The bus hissed to a stop and I saw a frizzy head retreat from the front row.

"I wonder what sport he plays," I said idly, watching Orren from the bus window.

"Who? Orren?" Justin peered out the window as the bus started up again. "He plays soccer. Wing. Pretty decent, too."

"Really?" I asked. For some reason, I found that kind of hard to believe.

The bus lurched to a stop. "This is us," Justin said, and I followed him off the bus. Justin walked to a bike rack and undid the lock on his blue ten-speed.

"You rode your bike to the bus stop?" I asked him. "It's only four blocks away."

The corners of Justin's mouth curled into a smile. "I was running a little late this morning—needed all the help I could get. Need a ride?"

I grinned. "On that thing? With you? No, thanks."

"Come on, I'm an excellent driver," he said, but I shook my head. "Have it your way. I'll see you tomorrow." He gave a little wave and rode off.

I sighed. Ugh, I thought, tomorrow. More middle-school fun.

"How did it go?" Mom asked the minute I walked into the kitchen.

"Don't ask." I grabbed a cookie.

Mom nodded and gave me a hug. "It's always hard to come back after the summer. Do you want to help me chop some veggies?" she asked, turning back to the counter.

I slung my book bag on the floor and said,

"Sure." I washed my hands and reached for the knife, peering at the open recipe on the counter. Veggie lasagna—one of my many faves. Mom hates cleaning, but she loves cooking. And that's the better deal, as far as I'm concerned. Plus, she runs her own design firm out of our house, so that means that she's always home to make dinner.

I washed some parsley and was just starting to chop it up when the phone rang. I pulled the receiver from the wall and cradled it against my shoulder while I chopped. Multitasking is a skill I've picked up from Mom, who is always doing about fifteen things at once.

"Allison, how's the new school going?" It was Dad's voice. Besides, he's the only person on the planet who calls me Allison.

"Oh—great," I lied. "I've got this really smart lab partner in science." Actually, that part was true. It turns out that Orren Kendall is a serious brain. He doesn't talk much, but he always seems to know the answers to everything.

Mom passed me a washed green pepper, and I sliced it in half.

"What about soccer?" Dad asked. "Is there a team?"

"Mmm," I said. I don't know why, but I just couldn't bring myself to tell Dad about practice. I guess I really was afraid that I wouldn't start. And then I'd have to tell him I was a benchwarmer. I just . . . didn't want to tell him. "I'm not so sure about that."

"Well, find out," Dad insisted. "Sports are a great way to make friends."

Yeah, as long as you don't stink, I added mentally.

"So, listen, I'm calling because I'm coming to town in a few weeks."

"You are?" I asked, putting down my knife. Dad comes through pretty regularly because of business—he's in sales. But still, only, like, once every couple of months. Lionel and I always have a great time when he comes over—it's way more fun than visiting Dad at his house. Dad is remarried to the most boring woman in the world. Marci and my dad bicker a lot, and when she's alone with me or Lionel, she can't talk about anything but my baby brother, Daniel, who is three.

Luckily, Daniel is really cute and funny. Otherwise I think I'd go crazy.

"Yeah, I was hoping that you and Lionel and I could go out to dinner."

"That would be great!" I said eagerly.

"So don't make any plans for Tuesday, October twenty-fourth. We're going out."

"Okay," I told him. "Give Daniel a kiss for me."

"Sure," Dad said. I knew I should ask to speak to Marci, but I just couldn't make myself do it. Luckily, Dad let it go. "Is Lionel there?"

"Oh, yeah, I'll go get him." I covered the receiver with my hand and turned to my mom. "Dad is coming on October twenty-fourth," I told her. "He wants to take me and Lionel out to dinner."

Mom rolled her eyes and frowned slightly. "You'd think he'd check with *me*," she grumbled, but she circled the date on the wall calendar and wrote, *Howard out w/kids.*

I ran up the stairs and busted into Lionel's room. He was lying on his bed, listening to his iPod, but he sat up when he saw me. "Get out!" he shouted.

"Dad's on the phone, tumbleweed-hair," I said, eyeing my brother's serious case of bed head. "I'll be happy to tell him that you're too busy to talk—"

Lionel grabbed the phone from my hand and pointed to the door. Then he turned his back on me. "Hey, Dad," he said into the receiver.

I stuck out my tongue at his back and went downstairs.

Dad is coming, I thought as I trotted down the steps, grinning. At least now I had something to look forward to.

pe•cool•iar \peh-'cool-yer\ *adj* : something (or someone) both cool and strange at the same time

"This microscope is defective." I pressed my
eye against the telescopey-thing and adjusted
the crank on the side. "Unless we're supposed to
be studying blurs."

"I think maybe you've got to adjust it the
other way," Orren said shyly.

I scooched back and let him take over.
He sort of slithered the slide around, then turned
the crank. Sighing, I looked over at Tam and
Renee. They were pointing to their microscope
and giggling. God—what is so funny about a
microscope? I wondered, gritting my teeth. I
glared at my microscope. Tell me a joke, I thought
at it. Be funny.

But the microscope didn't do anything.
Orren was still peering into it. "There you go," he
said finally, clearing the way for me.

I peeped in. "Hey," I said, "that looks like—something." Actually, what it looked like was one of my dad's blueberry pancakes. Kind of squiggly at the edges, and full of weird-looking blobs. "How did you do that?" I asked.

"I have a microscope at home," Orren admitted. "It was a Christmas present from my grandmother," he added quickly, which made things a little bit better. I mean, at least he hadn't saved up his allowance for it. "Want to see something cool?"

Hmm, I wonder what *cool* means in dorkese, I thought. I shrugged. "Okay."

Reaching up, he plucked one of the hairs from his frizzy head and placed it on a microscope slide. Then he adjusted the microscope and backed away. "Take a look."

I lifted my eyebrows at him. "That's not cool," I informed him. "That's gross."

"Yeah," Orren said, laughing and blushing slightly, "but check it out."

Well, I guess it could be some worse bodily product, I thought, leaning over to peer in.

I hate to say this, but that hair really was kind

of amazing. First of all, it didn't look like a hair. It looked more like a long, twisty pinecone, or a gnarled tree limb covered in rough bark.

"You know," Orren said, like it was perfectly normal that I was looking at a blown-up image of his hair, "if you shrunk the earth to the size of a pool ball, it would seem just as smooth as a pool ball is, and vice versa." This was typical Orren information. He'd started talking a lot more lately, and he was always saying things like: "If a lobster loses a claw or an eye, it can grow another," or "Slugs have four noses!" You know—interesting. But weird. He's one pecooliar dude, I decided.

A peal of laughter cut through the room. I looked up. It was Tam.

"Tamara," Mrs. Larsen said, "are you finished with your lab?" Her eye shadow was green today, and I found it extremely disturbing. Very Wicked Witch.

"Not quite," Tam replied in a sweet voice.

"Well, then. I suggest you quiet down and focus on your work."

Once Mrs. Larsen turned her back, Tam

swatted Renee on the arm, and the two bent over their lab work. But their shoulders were shaking with laughter. Jealousy slithered into my stomach and coiled there like a snake.

Just then, the bell rang, and I started packing up my bag. I felt a pang of relief as Tam hurried over with Renee dragging behind her. Part of me had worried that they might just walk off without me. Tam waited until Orren took off, then draped herself over my lab table. "I am so sorry that you're stuck with him," she said in this serious voice.

"He's not that bad," I said, thinking about how Orren had adjusted our microscope, and everything.

Renee cocked an eyebrow. "Not that bad? Please. All of his shirts are weird shades of green, and he likes Snoopy."

"And his hair makes him look like he just got hit by lightning," Tam added.

"You know, he actually put one of his hairs under the microscope," I confessed.

"Eewww!"

"Girls," Mrs. Larsen said, frowning at us from

the front of the room. "Don't you have to get to class?"

She was right—two minutes to the bell. I grabbed my book bag, and the three of us beat it out of there.

"Girls, I need you to leave so I can smear more green chalk dust on my eyelids," Renee cooed in this flutey voice once we were halfway down the hall.

Tam and I cracked up. I couldn't help it. Renee was just too good with a put-down.

———————

su•per•no•va \soo-per-'no-va\ *n.:* someone who's so hot, he could melt your brain just by standing near you

I could hear Coach Connors's voice in my mind— like an annoying echo—as I trotted over to the other practice fields to meet Tam. She still had me stuck on striker, and, again, I had missed a goal early on during practice. Then, since I didn't want to mess up anymore, I just kept passing to Jack. Jack didn't miss goals.

I thought I'd kind of played it off, but Coach took me aside after practice. "Kimball," she said, pinning me with those intense brown eyes, "you've got to get aggressive. Strikers strike."

That's why I want to sweep! I thought. Sweep!

"You've got the speed, and you've got the accuracy when you're passing," Coach went on. "You just need to work on your confidence." Then she squeezed me on the shoulder.

Like it was just that easy.

I needed to talk to Tam. This whole school was starting to get to me. But when I rounded the science building, I saw that the other practice fields were nearly empty. The guys' soccer team was packing up, and the cheer squad was nowhere to be seen.

I stood there for a while, totally confused. What happened? I wondered. Did Tam go home already? But I had talked to her at lunch, and she'd said that she would meet me after practice so we could ride the bus together. . . .

Looking around, I spotted Justin packing up his gear. "Hey," I called.

Justin looked up and grinned. "Hey!"

"You seen Tam?"

"Uh . . . I don't know." His face was a little red. Is he blushing? I wondered.

"She was supposed to meet me here," I said, trying not to smile. Does Justin have a little crush on Tam? I wondered. Is that why he's blushing?

"Oh, uh . . . wait a minute. Yeah. I think I saw her walking toward the parking lot with Renee." Justin shoved his cleats into his bag. "Why?"

"Oh . . . nothing," I hedged. Did Tam go home with Renee? I wondered. It sure sounded like it. I looked down at the friendship ring on my hand, feeling confused.

"Allie!" a voice called. I turned and saw Jack standing with Elena and Chris. My heart thudded in my chest in a very familiar way. Chris looked the same. Well . . . maybe a little more gorgeous.

I have no memory of walking over to join Jack and Elena, but I must have done it, because I found myself staring up into the golden flecks in Chris's blue eyes. He's such a supernova, I thought, feeling my face flush.

"Allie, this is my cousin Chris," Jack said.

For a moment, I wasn't sure that I'd understood what she said. "Your cousin?"

"My *baby* cousin." Jack grinned. "I'm two months older."

My head was swimming. Jack was Chris's cousin? But she didn't go to my elementary school. . . . Then again, why should she have? I wondered. She probably lived across town. I wish someone had clued me in earlier. "Hi," I said lamely.

"Hey," Chris said. His voice was velvety warm and soft.

"We're going out for ice cream," Elena piped up. "Do you want to come?"

I hesitated. On the one hand, eating ice cream with Chris was a bona fide dream come true. On the other hand, I thought of all of the things that could go wrong: I could spill something on myself, I could look like a pig, I could get a drip or a sprinkle on my face and not know it. . . . Besides, there was the whole Tam mystery. We were supposed to meet up—what if she was sitting on the bus, waiting for me? Actually, the thought made me a little panicky. She could be waiting right now, I realized, wondering where I am, and getting mad. "Sorry, guys," I said finally, "I have to pass."

"Next time," Jack suggested.

"Definitely," I told her.

"Hey, Allie, you coming?" Justin called.

"Yeah. Hold up a minute!" I turned back and said, "I'll see you guys later," but it was Chris I was looking at. I couldn't help it. I tried to tear my eyes away, but they wouldn't seem to go anywhere else.

"See you," Jack and Elena chorused as Chris gave me a nod.

I couldn't wait to tell Tam about this.

———◦———

men•tion•i•ac \'men-shun-ee-ak\ *n* : someone who keeps mentioning the same thing over and over and over . . .

"Mom!" I shouted as I walked in the door. "I'm ho—"

I bit off the last part of my sentence. There was chanting coming from the living room. I looked to the right and saw my mom, Mrs. Wilkerson from down the street, and Eileen Ohara—my mom's best friend—sitting cross-legged on the floor.

Grimacing, I tiptoed through the family

room toward the kitchen. I'd forgotten it was Wednesday. Yoga night.

Lionel grunted at me as I slung my backpack on the floor. I was starving, so I reached for the other half of his patriot. That's what we call an American cheese sandwich in my house. But he just slapped my hand away and sort of let out this growly snarl, so I headed for the fridge. I grabbed the orange juice and swigged from the carton.

Lionel watched me. "Do you know how many germs you carry in your mouth?"

"Do you know how many dorky facts you carry in your brain?" I retorted, taking another swig. I screwed the cap back on the OJ. "Did anyone call for me?" I asked, thinking of Tam. She hadn't been on the bus, after all. Mom always leaves a note on the fridge if anyone calls, but Lionel usually blows it off.

"Yeah, but I told the mental institution that I didn't know where you were," Lionel retorted. "You owe me one."

I rolled my eyes.

Just then, the chanting stopped, and some flute-and-chime music came on. Mom had picked up this CD at some world music fair, and said that it helped her "de-stress." Personally, it made me want to claw the walls. When I want to de-stress, I put on loud music and dance around my room like crazy. That tinkly stuff just drives me nuts.

"Downward-facing dog." I could hear Mom's voice from the other room. She's been taking yoga classes since she was a kid in the 1970s, and she gets up and does her routine every morning. Now she teaches an informal class on Wednesday for any of her friends who want to learn. "That's good, Helen," she told Mrs. Wilkerson. "Now bend your knees and give a big stretch back. Good. Now, three-point. Lift your right leg."

I heard a grunt, then a thud as Mrs. Wilkerson toppled over.

Lionel sighed. "Why can't I live in a normal family?" he asked the ceiling. Then he trudged out of the room.

I grabbed an apple and followed him. "Hey, Peebles," I said to my cat, who was curled up on my bed, asleep. I leaned over her and gave her a kiss on the head, then stroked the fur between her ears. Peebles gave a sleepy "Brrowr . . ." and shifted slightly, but she didn't open her eyes. She's kind of lazy, but I love her anyway.

Settling down at my desk, I booted up my computer and crunched into the sweet tartness of my apple. I checked my e-mail. There was a "Welcome to the Tigers" e-mail from Coach Connors. I skimmed the e-mail, which gave a list of names and phone numbers of the team members, as well as a schedule of games and practices. But there was nothing from Tam. She wasn't on my IM buddy list, either, so I decided to give her a call.

She picked up on the third ring. "Hello?"

"Tam? It's Allie."

"Hey! How was practice?"

"Great. How 'bout you?"

"Oh, it was so fun," Tam said brightly. "We're making up a new cheer, and the coach came up with this really cool move where—okay, we stand in a group of three, and two people plant their feet and flip the third one over. I'm one of the people who gets flipped. I keep ending up with my hair in my face, but I think it's going to look really great when we work out the kinks."

"Sounds cool," I said, and it really did. Of course, if I ever tried a move like that, I'd end up with gravel permanently implanted in my face. But that's why I'm a soccer player, not a cheerleader. "Just wear your hair in a ponytail."

"Yeah," Tam agreed. "That's what Renee said she was going to do."

"So, uh, did practice get out early, or something?" I asked, trying to ignore Renee's name. Tam was becoming a bit of a mentioniac when it came to Renee, and it was starting to bug me. "I looked for you before I got on the bus. . . ."

"Oh, yeah. Renee said that her mom could take us home after practice, so I just went with her," Tam said, like we'd never made plans to hang out together or anything.

I was starting to think that maybe we *hadn't* made plans. I mean, maybe I'd misunderstood. Maybe it was just an *I'll catch you later* kind of deal. I didn't want to blow the whole thing out of proportion. Besides, we were hanging out right now, kind of. "So, uh, I rode home on the bus with Justin." I kicked off my shoes and lay back against my pile of pillows. "I think he has a megacrush on someone."

"Who?" Tam asked. She loves gossip.

"Someone whose name rhymes with Stamara Stompson."

"Me?" Tamara squealed. "Really? How do you know?"

"He asks about you a lot." Besides, I added mentally, every guy has a crush on you. I nudged Peebles with my foot. She meowed in protest, then got up. Stepping onto my stomach, she tucked herself, sphinxlike, onto my belly. "So, what do you think?"

Giggling, Tam admitted, "He's okay. Kind of short. But there's lots of cute guys at Cleveland. Especially the older ones."

"Mmm," I said, even though I didn't think Justin was short at all. He was at least two inches taller than Tam. But it didn't seem worth arguing about, so I just changed the subject. "Guess who I talked to at boys' soccer practice today."

"Who?"

"Chris Gibson."

"Ohmygosh," Tam said. "Did he ask you for a pen?"

"Ha, ha."

Tamara giggled. "Just kidding. So—was he as cute as ever?"

"Supernova," I said, grinning. Peebles stared at me with calm yellow eyes, as if this conversation was way below her intelligence. Which maybe it was. "He's my friend Jack's cousin."

"Who's Jack? Is he cute, too?"

I laughed. "Well, I guess you could say that, but Jack is a girl. She's on the soccer team."

"Oh," Tam said. "A Sweaty Betty." That was what a lot of kids called the Tigers, but there was something about the way Tam said it that kind of made it sound like she was wrinkling her nose or something.

"*I'm* a Sweaty Betty," I said, kind of hurt.

"Well, yeah, but you're normal."

I stared at the receiver. "What's that supposed to mean?"

"Oh, nothing. It's just that all of those Cleveland soccer girls are, like, superjocks."

"That's why they win," I told her.

"I guess." Tam didn't sound convinced.

Just then, there was a knock at my door and Mom stuck her head into my room. "Oof," I said as Peebles jumped off my belly and darted through between Mom's feet and into the hallway. "Hold on," I said to Tam.

"Sweetie, dinner is in five minutes," Mom said.

"Okay," I told Mom. "I'll be down in a sec. Tam?" I said into the phone. "I've gotta go. Dinner."

"Okay," Tam said. "I'll see you tomorrow."

"Okay, see you on the bus," I said. "Bye." I clicked the OFF button and hauled myself off the bed toward the bathroom. But I paused in front of my bookcase.

I couldn't stop myself. I pulled down the old LFC notebook. I had to flip through it for a minute, but eventually I found the page I was looking for.

Reasons Allie likes Chris G.
1. His blue eyes
2. His blond hair
3. He has a nice smile
4. Seems smart

I snapped closed the notebook and put it back on the shelf. All of those things are still true, I told myself. Chris was exactly the same.

And so was my crush on him.

- 5 -

pre•dork•a•ment \ pre-'dork-a-ment \ *n* : a real
dilemma—but only if you're a nerd—*see* NORK

Orren's eyebrows drew together in concentration as he used the small dropper to drip ammonia into a beaker of lavender-colored cabbage water. It was Thursday, lab day, and we were studying acids and bases. I sighed as he stared at our experiment, as though he thought he could make it do something interesting using the power of his mind.

But all that happened was that the liquid turned yellowish. Orren dipped a piece of pH paper into the liquid. Green. "Write that down," he commanded.

I rolled my eyes and obeyed. I let Orren do the labs because he was good at them, even though it drove me crazy that he was so slow and perfect about it. I was way too impatient to do the experiments correctly. Like when we had to study polymers. I just dropped the sodium borate and the guar gum in the water and mixed it all up without waiting the exact amount of time between steps. When Orren complained, I'd said, "Hey—it's only science. It's not an exact science." Which Orren found infuriating.

After that particular experiment—which ended up producing liquidy goo instead of slime—Orren announced that he would do the labs, and I could write them up, which was fine with me. I had an easier time with writing than Orren did. He labored over every sentence, while words flowed out of me.

Just then, there was a giggle at the front of the class. Renee had put a piece of litmus paper in her mouth, and Tam was laughing as though that were the funniest thing that she had ever seen in her entire life. I glared at Renee, hoping that litmus paper tasted like barf.

Do I sound annoyed?

It just didn't seem fair that Tam and Renee were lab partners. After all, they already had four other classes together.

"Allie?" Orren peered at me from under

his Brillo-pad hair. "It's another base."

I was so zoned out that for a minute I actually thought he was talking sports. Then I remembered where we were, and scribbled the latest results on my notebook paper.

"Okay, that's it," Orren said. "I'll clean up while you get the results together."

I nodded and started copying what we had done onto a fresh sheet of paper as Tam let out a laughing shriek. Renee had dripped some goopy liquid soap on Tam's arm.

"Ladies," Mrs. Larsen said sharply, "do I need to separate you two?"

Hope squiggled through my body like milk through a curly straw. If they got separated, maybe I could be Tam's lab partner.

Tam and Renee looked sheepish, and muttered "No, ma'am." I noticed that they were only on vinegar, the fourth experiment in the lab. There were twelve in all. They were going to have to hurry if they wanted to finish.

There was a soft knock on the door, and Mr. Sykes, our social studies teacher, poked his head in. "Hi, everyone!" he said brightly. "I hope you don't mind if I borrow your teacher for a few minutes. Linda?"

"Sure, Clarence," Mrs. Larsen said. I've always thought that hearing your teachers use each others' first names is completely freakish. "Class, when you're finished, please place your labs face down on my desk." Then Mrs. Larsen stepped out of the room.

Once she was gone, the class was completely silent . . . for about ten seconds. The sound built almost like an avalanche—the way the first little rock tumbles down, then the next, then a few more. . . . Suddenly the whole class was chattering away, and David Cho and Randy Jefferson had gone up to the blackboard to play hangman.

From my seat behind them, I could see that Tam and Renee were looking at a magazine. Orren was nearby at the slop sink, scrubbing out our beakers. Oh, well, I thought. It's probably better that Orren doesn't want to play games or act stupid. At least I'll get this lab done. I put the finishing touches on it just as Orren got back to our table.

"Basic Training for Acids," he read aloud over my shoulder. "Good title." He scanned the rest of the lab, and nodded. "Looks great."

I smiled dubiously. "You think?" I'd sort of expected him to wig out when he saw the title. But Orren had loosened up lately.

"Sure." Orren nodded at the paper. "Hand it in."

I smiled at him, and he smiled back. That was when I noticed something weird. I'd always thought that Orren's eyes were brown, but they weren't. They were dark green. It's just that you couldn't really tell, because his frizzy hair hid half of his face.

Plucking the paper from his hand, I headed up the center aisle toward Mrs. Larsen's desk. Just before I reached it, someone grabbed my hand.

"Hey!" I said, smiling brightly when I saw it was Tam. She didn't look happy. "What's wrong?"

"Allie, there's only three minutes until the bell," Tam said.

"I know." I looked over at Renee. "Do

you guys need some help with the lab?"

"We don't have time," Tam said. "I don't know what happened, we just, kind of lost track of time, and . . ." Tam glanced at the paper in my other hand.

Renee cut to the chase. "Can we borrow your lab?"

I stood there for a moment, feeling like something heavy had just whizzed past my head. Borrow my lab? She meant *copy*. My jaw tightened. Tam knows I've hated cheating ever since Tommy Samuelson copied my spelling test in the third grade, and when we both flunked, he went around telling everyone that I couldn't spell. Part of me couldn't believe she was even asking. Plus, I felt kind of mad. I mean, I'd been working all period—having a very boring time—while they'd been goofing around having fun. I ask you, is that fair?

Besides, this wasn't just my lab. It was Orren's lab, too. I didn't feel like I could just hand it over.

"Please," Tam whispered. She glanced at the door. "Before she comes back."

I looked down at Tam's hand in mine. Our fingers were interlaced, and our friendship rings were right next to each other. Oh man, I thought, what's the huge predorkament here? Just hand over the lab.

Glancing back at Orren, I saw that he was busily copying down the homework assignment. "Just don't let anyone see," I whispered as I slipped Tam the paper.

"Thanks," Tam said gratefully. "I owe you."

Renee smiled at me.

I headed back to my seat, feeling kind of glad that I'd handed over the paper. It was weird how doing the wrong thing actually kind of felt like doing the right thing.

I guess that's the way things work in middle school.

———————◆———————

an•em•o•ne \an-'em-o-nee\ *n* : someone who isn't exactly an enemy, but is just sort of hanging out, waiting to sting you

"Hey!" I said as I slid my lunch tray across the table next to Tam's.

"Allie!" Tam grinned, gesturing to the seat

next to hers. "Thanks so much for saving us today."

"Yeah, be sure to thank Orren for me," Renee said with a smirk. "And tell him that I think he's hot." Renee was really starting to annoy me. No *Thank you, Allie*, just a big old insult for my lab partner. She's such an anemone. "Why are you laughing?" Renee asked Tamara, who was giggling so hard that I thought ketchup was going to come out of her nose. "I'm totally serious. He's gorgeous. Stop laughing, I mean it!"

Tam was losing it.

"Hey, Tam," Renee went on. "Maybe we could double date. Me and Orren, and you and your boyfriend over there." She nodded toward this really overweight guy in the corner. He was eating green Jell-O. I don't know, something about the scene made me laugh a little, too, even though I felt bad about it.

"I don't know," Tam said, catching her breath. "I'm thinking of breaking up with him. I'm totally crushing on that guy at the head of the cafeteria line."

Renee and I both turned to look. The

guy was tall and skinny, and when he stepped forward, his movements were all jerky, like a marionette.

"Ooh, didn't I see him in *CosmoGIRL* magazine?" Renee joked, plucking a French fry from my plate. "As one of the Top Hotties? Hey, Allie, maybe you should go for Mr. Forks and Knives, over there."

I didn't even turn around—I knew who she was talking about. I could feel the smile wavering on my face. When we took our empty trays to the back of the cafeteria, there was a guy who collected our silverware and dropped it into a washtub. He had a flat face and close-set, almond-shaped eyes. I'm pretty sure he had Down syndrome.

I don't know; it seemed really wrong to make fun of him. But Tam and Renee were laughing, and I knew that if I said anything, I'd just sound like some kind of public-service announcement and they would tell me to chill out.

"I think I need a soda," I said, wanting to get out of there.

"Let us know if you spot any hotties," Renee said as I stood up.

"Yeah, don't go stealing our boyfriends!" Tam added.

I smiled weakly and headed toward the vending machine, hoping that they would have changed the subject by the time I got back. I arrived at the snack machines just in time to see Jack nearby with Elena . . . and Chris in all of his gorgeousness. I stopped in my tracks and nearly turned right around, but I was a split second too late.

"Allie!" Elena had spotted me.

"Hey!" Jack chimed in, waving. "Over here!"

"Oh, hey!" I said, as though I totally hadn't realized they were there. My heart was pounding in my ears. Act casual, I told myself as I walked over to their table. "Hey, guys," I said to Jack and Elena. "Hey, Chris," I said, all cool, like I just happened to remember his name.

"Sit down," Jack urged.

I plopped into a chair next to her, and directly across from Chris. I had an incredible view of his gorgeous blue eyes. Say something brilliant! I commanded myself. But what?

"Think you'll start in the game next week?" Jack asked me.

"I hope," I confessed, "but I doubt it. There's plenty of girls better than me."

"Lies," Elena said. "Allie's a great player," she informed Chris.

A burning sensation crept up the back of my neck, and I knew I was blushing again. That's a big problem for me. I blush all the time. "So, what's for lunch?"

"Don't ask me," Jack said, "I'm only eating the Tater Tots."

"They're just an excuse to eat ketchup," Elena said. "My favorite vegetable."

I turned to Chris. "Those fish sticks look delicious," I said sarcastically. They were covered in green glop. "Enjoying them?"

"Not really," Chris said seriously. "They aren't that good."

I sat there for a minute, wishing that I had a napkin to hide behind. He didn't get my joke, I realized. He must think I'm an idiot. And then I felt myself blushing again.

I opened my mouth to explain that I was

kidding, but Elena jumped in and said, "Personally, I really like to *savor* the cafeteria food. The complicated flavors are really . . ." She trailed off, searching for the right word.

"Revolting?" Jack guessed.

"That's it," Elena said, nodding.

"Like the desserts, for example," I agreed, joining the joke. "It takes a refined palate to enjoy just how bad butterscotch pudding can be."

Everyone cracked up, except for Chris. "I like the pudding," he said.

Oh. My. GOD! My jokes were bouncing off him like bullets off of Superman's chest! I felt like such an utter nork. Just then, the bell rang. I looked up at the clock, thinking, Fire drill? But no—lunch was over. I'd spent the whole time chatting with Jack and her gang—I hadn't even eaten anything! "I'll see you guys later," I said, shoving back my chair.

"See you," Jack said.

I hurried across the cafeteria to collect my backpack. I couldn't wait to tell Tam that I had just spent all of lunch hanging with Chris! But when I got back to the lunch table, Renee and Tam had already left. Only my tray and my book bag were there.

And to make things worse, someone had eaten all of my fries. Renee sure does have a big mouth, I thought bitterly, in more ways than one.

style-o-me•ter \'stile-o-mee-tr\ *n* : a measurement indicating just how fashionable you are—or, you know, are not

Soccergrl228: Hey! What ru up 2 2day?

tamtam14: family junk. Grandma. U?

Soccergrl228: oh, same. Have to help Mom with some stuff. Call me later?

tamtam14: won't be back until 2nite. Call u tomorrow?

Soccergrl228: cool. Bye. Have fun at Grandma's!

I stared at the blinking cursor on my computer monitor, feeling oddly empty, like a toothpaste tube that's been all squeezed out. It was Saturday, and I had nothing to do. There wasn't even anyone I could call. It seemed too weird to call some of my old friends from elementary school. Especially since it was so last minute. I couldn't see myself calling Julie or Mandy and saying, "Hey, I know we haven't talked since before the summer, but I was wondering if you wanted to go see a movie in half an hour." The only person I could be that last minute with was Tam, because we spent almost every Saturday together. We didn't even have to make plans. Those were the plans.

But not today. Peebles, who was standing on my windowsill, let out a jaw-breaking yawn and then stretched until she was about a yard long, with her butt in the air. Then she sat down and gazed out the window. She looked as bored as I felt.

"I guess it's just you and me," I said to the cat. "And my school books." Oh, man, I thought. Am I seriously considering doing schoolwork on a Saturday? That's just sad.

I laced my fingers together and rested my chin on them, feeling a strange sense of cold anger in my stomach—as if I'd swallowed a whole Popsicle. I wasn't really sure why, though. Tam couldn't help it if she had to go visit her grandma. I was mad at myself—mad that I hadn't checked to make sure we had plans. But I was also kind of mad at Tam. She should have told me that she wasn't going to be around. I felt kind of blown off.

"Allie?" Mom poked her head into my room.

"Yeah?" I didn't pick up my head from my desk.

Mom held up her keys and gave them a jingle. "I was going to go to the mall. I need a new skirt. Is there anything you need?"

I thought for a minute. "Some new cleats?" The sole on one of my old ones was starting to separate from the front of the shoe. It had tripped me up in practice a couple of times, and we had our first game next week.

"You want to come with me?" Mom asked.

I shrugged. "Sure," I said. "Just give me a minute."

Mom smiled, like she was really surprised. She knows that going to the mall is my idea of torture. But what the heck? I didn't have anything else to do . . . aside from social studies. "Take your time," Mom said. "I'll be downstairs."

I peeled off my pjs and went to wash my face and brush my teeth, deciding to skip the shower. It's Saturday, what do I need to be clean for? I thought, although I did go for some deodorant. I pulled on my oldest, softest jeans and my navy Yale sweatshirt (a present from Dad, who went there), slipped on my scuffed brown clogs, and yanked my hair into a bushy ponytail. Good enough, I decided as I looked in the mirror. You know, for the mall.

---

fash•ion pas•sion \fash-un-pash-un\ *n* : the kind of mania that comes over you when you are trying on clothes in a dressing room, and convinces you that you should immediately buy everything that isn't nailed down

The mall was just starting to get busy as Mom and I walked in at the second level. We started out in one of Mom's favorite boutiques. I waited in an overstuffed chair while Mom tried on a few skirts. She looked great in everything, of course. Mom is funny, because she's kind of a casual person, but she has a lot of dress-up clothes. She always looks really nice, even when she's just wearing her yoga pants and a fleecy pullover. And whenever she has to meet people for work, she gets dressed up in suits and high heels with a matching purse and junk like that. It's almost like she was born with some good-clothes gene, or something. Tamara is the same way. I'm not.

I looked down at my old sweatshirt and ancient jeans that hadn't been washed in about three weeks. This is what I mean, I thought. This is my favorite outfit.

"What do you think of this, Allie?" Mom held out a sweater knit from blue and purple chunky yarn. "Want to try it?"

"Okay." Standing up, I yanked off my sweat-shirt and pulled the sweater over my T-shirt. It was so soft—like being wrapped in a baby blanket, or a cloud, or something.

"That looks great." Mom spun me, so I could see myself in the full-length mirror.

"Wow," I said. The sweater did look good. I usually wear really baggy clothes, but this was a little more form-fitting—just enough so that you could see my waist. It had a V-neck and bell sleeves, and the color made my hair look more vibrant, and my brown eyes look really rich.

It's funny, I thought. This is the kind of sweater that Tam would wear.

I looked over at Mom, who was now frowning at my jeans. "I really like this sweater, Mom," I told her.

"Great—sold. Allie, sweetheart . . . maybe we should get you some more new clothes." Mom lifted her eyebrows, like she half expected me to tell her to get lost.

I turned back to face myself in the mirror, taking in my faded jeans with the hole in the knee and my scuffed-up shoes that looked like they'd been run over by a tractor. I was scoring about a negative one zillion on the style-o-meter. "You think I should get *new* clothes, when I've already got great outfits like this one?" I joked.

The edges of Mom's eyes crinkled up into a smile.

"Okay," I said, pulling the sweater over my head. "Let's do some shopping."

"I can't believe you talked me into buying a skirt," I said as Mom and I walked out of store number five zillion, three hours later.

"Two skirts," Mom corrected.

"Ohmygosh," I said, peering down at the

shopping bags in my hands. "I'd forgotten about the black one." Mom had helped me pick out a really pretty outfit—a hot-pink blouse and a long black skirt—for the sports banquet. I stopped in my tracks, biting my lip and feeling like a victim of fashion passion. "Maybe we should take one back," I said uncertainly.

Mom laughed. "The corduroy one isn't exactly a dress-up skirt."

"That's true," I admitted. I guess I was just feeling sort of overwhelmed by the sheer amount of stuff we'd bought. In addition to the two skirts and the blue sweater, I'd picked out a new pair of jeans, two funky pairs of pants—one pair of red plaid low-riders and a maroon velvet pair—two more sweaters, three shirts, a pair of chunky black boots, a completely cool pair of red suede sneaks, and yes, the cleats. Oh, and a new black backpack. We'd already had to go back to the car twice to dump stuff in the trunk.

"Okay," Mom said, scanning the stores nearby. "Is there anything else you need? A winter coat? Hats? A raincoat?"

Mom said something else, but suddenly her

voice blurred with the background noise of the busy mall. Because that was when I saw them. Tam and Renee. They were coming out of a store, giggling.

I froze.

"Allie?" Mom said, turning. She had walked a few steps ahead. "What's wrong?" She turned to where I was looking. "Isn't that Tam? Do you want to say hi?"

I felt light-headed, like I couldn't get enough air. I pressed my hand against my stomach, which felt nauseatingly hollow. "No," I said quickly.

Mom's eyebrows flew up.

"I——I don't want her to see my new clothes," I hedged. "I want to surprise her on Monday."

Mom looked like she didn't believe me, but I didn't feel like explaining that Tam had lied to me. Lied, so she could hang with Renee instead of me.

"It's okay," Mom said gently. We stood there for a moment, until Tam and Renee walked into another store. She wrapped an arm around my shoulder. "Let's go get some food. You'll feel better."

"Yeah," I mumbled, even though I wasn't

hungry anymore. The hollow feeling in the pit of my stomach stayed there.

Mom kissed me on the head. "It's okay," she whispered again into my ponytail.

But it wasn't.

---

dis•pos-a-friend \ dis-'poze-a-frend \ *n* : someone easily tossed away, like a used Kleenex

I lay on my bed, absently stroking Peebles's fur. She was curled into a tight ball at my waist. Shopping bags were piled next to my bed, two of them propped on my desk chair. I hadn't unpacked a single thing. I couldn't motivate to move.

Why had she lied to me? I thought over and over. Why had she ditched me? Had I done something? Said something? Or was it just that Tam liked Renee better?

I remembered the time Janine Jackson had called me a pig in fourth grade. Tam got the whole class on my side, and Janine finally apologized to me out by the swings, so everyone could hear.

That's what it was like—having Tam as my

best friend. I felt safe. But now, I felt kind of like a dispos-a-friend.

I held up my right hand. The blue friendship ring sat there as always. Pulling it off for a moment, I noticed how pale the skin was beneath the band. I hadn't taken it off since the day I first got it.

"We have to promise to wear these all the time," Tam had said the day we bought the rings. After we left the store, we went to our favorite spot in the park—the sunny side of the hill near the picnic tables. We were lying on our backs, looking up at the clouds. "Then, whenever we look at them, we'll think of each other."

I had looked at Tam. There was a blade of brilliant green grass caught in her curly black hair, but I didn't bother picking it out. It looked kind of pretty there. "We'll be friends forever," I said.

"Best friends," Tam agreed.

But now . . .

The phone rang, snapping me out of my trance. For a minute, I didn't move. Then I got this crazy idea that it might be Tam. A split-second image of how great it would be to say *Get lost* flashed through my mind, so I put my ring back on my finger, hauled myself off my bed, and picked it up.

"Hello?"

"Allie? It's Jack."

Jack? I was so surprised that for a moment, I didn't say anything.

"From soccer," Jack explained.

I laughed. "I only know one girl named Jack," I said. "Sorry, I was just—in the middle of something. What's up?"

"Do you want to hang out in the park and kick the ball around?"

I heard a mental echo of Tam's voice from the time when I had told her about Jack and she had said, "Oh, a Sweaty Betty," like she was sneering, and for a moment I hesitated. But then I decided, Oh, that's stupid. You're going to sit around alone because Jack is a jockissima? Jack is fun and I like soccer, and Tam is busy hanging with her snobalicious friend, anyway. "Uh—sure," I said finally. "When?"

"How soon can you get there?" Jack replied.

bore•chid \ 'bor-kid \ *n:* someone who looks good, but doesn't have much personality—they're just there for show, like an orchid, or some other pretty flower

Twenty minutes later, I jogged onto the playing field at the edge of the park. I had exchanged my scrungy jeans for an equally scrungy pair of shorts, and was wearing my new cleats.

"Allie!"

I turned toward the voice and was surprised to see Justin rolling toward me on his bike. "Hey!" I called. "What are you doing here?"

"Meeting up with you to play some soccer," Justin said, squeaking to a stop. "Chris called me." Justin jutted his chin and I looked behind me.

Sure enough, Jack was walking toward me . . . with Chris, Sally, and Tom Fine. I didn't really know Tom, but I knew who he was—he'd been Chris's best friend for years. He was kind of cute, but he never really talked much—I'd always thought he was kind of a borechid. What is he doing here? I thought as the group headed toward me and Justin. What is *Chris* doing here?

My heart nearly stopped. What is the deal

with today? I wondered frantically. Is this National Don't Tell Allie Stuff Day, or something? Miserably, I thought about all of the cute outfits piled on the floor of my room. And Chris has to see me in my holy, moldy Yale sweatshirt? Not that I would really have showed up to play soccer in my new maroon velvet pants, but still. I might have combed my hair.

Jack waved and trotted over. "How about girls against guys?" she called.

Justin shrugged. "Why don't we mix it up?"

Jack grinned. "Okay—Sally, Chris, and Allie against you, me, and Tom."

"Fine." Justin grinned. "As long as Allie doesn't mind getting beat."

My brain had barely processed anything after the words *Chris and Allie*, but I managed to trot onto the field after Chris.

"I'll be goalie," Sally volunteered.

"I'll cover defense," Chris said. "Allie, you can handle the top of the field."

Great. I needed the practice, anyway. I was starting to accept the fact that Coach Connors wasn't going to switch my position. Her two star strikers had graduated the year before, and she needed a fast runner in that position. Jack started out with the ball, and shot a quick pass to Justin, who headed toward our goal. Diving in, Chris made a quick steal, then side-kicked the ball to me. Nice move. I dribbled it up the field, trying not to wonder whether the way I ran looked stupid or not.

Chris cut away from Justin, and was open for a split second. But I felt really weird kicking it to him . . . I don't know, like I didn't want him to know that I was paying such close attention to him, or something. So I kicked the ball toward the goal.

Justin slapped it away like he was shooing a fly from a piece of pie. Easy.

"What was that?" Chris demanded. "I was open!"

"Sorry!" I called, wincing. Okay, he's your teammate, I told myself. You're *supposed* to be paying attention to him.

Justin tossed the ball back into play, and Jack took it. After a while, I managed to ease into the game. Chris became just another player, almost like a shadow. In the end, I gave him a few solid passes, and managed to score a point on Justin— the only point of the game.

"This stinks," Justin complained once the game was over. "I demand a rematch."

"Let's go for another half an hour," Jack suggested.

Sounds good to me, I thought, as I snuck a glance at Chris. Personally, I could play all day, as long as he was on my team!

I wracked my brain for something clever to say as Chris and I took the field again, but drew a total blank. Oh, well, I thought. Does it really matter? Chris and I are playing soccer!

That was way better than asking me for a pen.

- 7 -

Dweeb•o•saur•us rex \ 'dweeb-o-saur-us 'reks \ *n*
[Fr. Latin *dweebus maximus* major loser and *rex* king]
1: emperor of the nerds. **2**: a geek large enough and
out-of-control enough to inspire fear in others

I walked down the hall thinking, What was I thinking? My stupid new corduroy skirt was ruining my morning.

I should've changed. I knew it the minute I walked into the kitchen. Lionel took one look at me and nearly snorted a Froot Loop out of his nose.

"Lionel!" Mom glared at him. Then she smiled at me. "Allie, you look so pretty!"

Lionel coughed, still laughing through his breakfast cereal.

"That's it," I said, turning to hurry back up the stairs. I should've known that wearing a skirt would make me look stupid. ·

"No—wait," Mom called. "Allie, you have to be at the bus stop in three minutes."

I checked my watch. She was right. I was stuck in this dumb outfit. I mean, I'd really liked this outfit when I bought it, and I couldn't wait to put it on right away. But now it was looking like I'd made a major mistake.

"Oh, are we going to school?" Lionel asked. "I thought maybe we were going to church."

"They wouldn't let you in without an exorcism," I snapped, grabbing an apple.

"At least I'm not dressed like it's Halloween," Lionel shot back.

"Right—that's just your normal face, I forgot."

"Kids." Mom gave us this *Stop it right now!* frown. "It's late."

I sighed, and gave Mom a kiss on the cheek. Then I grabbed my lunch and my new black backpack and headed out the door.

Lionel and I didn't speak on the way to the bus stop. Which was fine with me. My stomach was squirming around like the inside of a dormant volcano that's about to erupt.

Wait a minute. Did I just think that? Whoa. That was very Orren.

Anyway, my stomach was queasy. I hadn't talked to Tam all weekend. She had never called after she went to see her "grandmother." I was kind of hoping to see her at the bus stop so we could make up and she could say something nice about my skirt so I wouldn't feel like such a Dweebosaurus rex, but she wasn't there.

Tam still wasn't there when the bus chugged and hissed to the curb. I trudged aboard slowly, hoping she would show up. I almost told the driver to wait, but then I remembered that I was mad at her, and just drooped into my seat and glared out the window.

The bus started to pull away, and I bit my lip. Could Tam be sick? Maybe something awful had happened. . . .

Oh, what do you care? another part of my brain screamed. Let her miss the bus.

But my heart was beating hard, and when someone banged on the side of the bus, I heaved a sigh of relief. I arranged my face into a frown as we jerked to a stop and the doors hissed open. I wanted Tam to know that I was mad.

"Thanks, Mrs. Lipscomb!" a cheery voice

called as the late passenger scrambled aboard. "I could never make it to school without you."

I rolled my eyes. It wasn't Tam. It was Justin.

"Hey!" Justin said brightly as he sort of flopped into the chair in front of me. "Where's Tam?"

"Good question."

"Oh my God," Justin said, eyeing my outfit. "Is it Picture Day?"

"I just felt like wearing a skirt," I snapped. "Why is that such a big deal?"

Justin held up his hands in mock surrender. "Sorry, sorry. It's just not something you see, you know . . . ever. It looks . . . nice," he added lamely, but it was too late. I snorted.

He sank into his chair in confusion and I scowled out the window for the rest of the ride.

So those were the cheerful memories of my morning that flashed through my brain as I walked down the hall toward my locker.

Someone put a light hand on my shoulder, and I jumped.

"Ohmygosh, Allie!" Tam said, spinning me around and giving me a huge smile. "You look great! Wow—cool new backpack," she added, checking it out. "I almost didn't recognize you."

Ugh. Was that supposed to be a compliment? "Thanks," I snapped. "Missed you on the bus."

"Oh, Renee and I are carpooling now," Tam explained. "Her mom takes us to school, and my mom picks us up after practice. It's way better than the bus," she added, rolling her eyes.

Thanks for telling me! I thought. Rage started to bubble in my chest. "Hmm," I grunted, fuming. "So—did you have a good time with your grandma this weekend?"

"Yeah," Tam said smoothly. "So, uh, where did these clothes come from?"

I folded my arms across my chest. "From the mall," I said, my voice dripping poison, "on Saturday."

I think I've told you that I blush at basically anything. Well, Tam is the opposite. She never blushes . . . but she was blushing now. "Oh." Her voice was a squeaky sigh.

"Yeah. I saw you there." My voice was wavering, but I forced myself to go on. "Why didn't you just tell me the truth?" I swallowed hard, annoyed with myself. I wanted to be angry, but now that Tam was standing in front of me, I just felt hurt.

Tam turned an even brighter shade of red. "It's just—I know you hate the mall," she said in a rush. "You know, you usually just wear whatever and dress like a guy—"

"Thanks," I snapped. Accidiss? I wondered. Or deliberadiss?

Tam winced. "Sorry," she said. "But, you know—what I mean." She cleared her throat and went on. "So when Renee asked if I wanted to go shopping, I thought, well, I'd better not tell Allie because she might feel like she has to come along, and then she'll be miserable. So I just made up a story. . . ." Tam's voice trailed off. "I was worried you'd be mad."

"I was mad," I told her. "I am mad."

Her dark eyes clouded over. "Well, I'm *sorry*, but you hate shopping."

I ask you—is that the point? But I didn't have time to say that out loud, because the bell rang.

"Fine," I said. The truth was, I just wanted this conversation to be over so that things could go back to normal with me and Tam. "Apology accepted," I added, even though I wasn't really sure that Tam had apologized.

"Good." Tam's serious face broke into a smile. "And you really do look great."

Not like a guy? I thought. But I didn't say that. What I said was, "See you in science."

Tam nodded. "See you."

Now I only had four minutes to get to my locker and homeroom. I turned to hurry down the hall, but just as I did, the world jolted. Literally. Flailing like a crazed Tickle Me Elmo doll, I tripped and fell face-first onto the fake-granite hall floor.

I looked behind me accusingly to get a look at the guilty foot. Someone's toes were about to get stepped on.

"Allie? I'm so sorry!" Chris, who had been crouching to peer into his bottom locker, stood up and rushed over to help me. "Sorry about that," he repeated as I straightened my clothes. "Jack always says that I have huge feet." He gave me an apologetic smile.

My heart went bonkers. "Oh, well," I said

breathlessly, "maybe you have a future as a clown."

Chris looked confused. "I'm really more into math and stuff."

I giggled nervously as my face flushed. Didn't he realize that was a joke?

"I like your sweater," Chris said.

Say thank you! I commanded myself. But the words wouldn't come out.

The one-minute warning rang.

"Well, I guess I'll see you later." Chris turned and headed down the hall.

"See you." My voice was a whisper, and I knew Chris hadn't heard me as he disappeared into his homeroom. Oh, well, I thought as I turned and hurried toward my class. At least he liked my outfit.

Mil•ky Way \'mil-kee 'way\ *n* : someone who looks hard on the outside, but actually has a soft marshmallow center

"So the pH blah-blahdy-blah . . ." Mrs. Larsen was droning on once again. Her voice has this strange quality; sometimes it sounds like a vacuum cleaner.

My eyes were open, but I could hardly concentrate on her words.

Orren, on the other hand, was staring at her like she was spewing the secrets of the universe, writing down every word.

I tuned back in once Mrs. Larsen looked up at the clock. "We only have a few minutes left, so I'm going to pass back the labs from the other day. Most of you did very well." Picking up a stack of papers, Mrs. Larsen started walking around the room. She whispered something to each pair of students as she handed over the papers.

I drummed my fingers on the black marble lab table, feeling antsy. "Nice work," she whispered as she handed the paper back to Stephen and Vickie, who sat in front of us.

I sat up straighter, eager to see how we had done.

The smile dropped from Mrs. Larsen's face as she handed me the paper. "Please see me after class," she said in this weird robot voice.

My stomach soured. Oh, no.

Orren frowned and looked at me. "What did she say?" he asked.

"She said we should see her after class," I told him. I flipped over the paper, and there it was. A big red zero.

"Zero?" Orren's face turned white. "My parents are going to kill me."

I could feel myself blushing like a tomato. I swallowed hard, but I just couldn't bear to tell him that this was all my fault.

Why do I have to be so lousy at cheating when everyone else is so good at it?

The bell rang and Orren and I trudged to the front of the room while everyone started buzzing and thumping books closed, gathering things for their next class. Renee and Tam were already standing by Mrs. Larsen's desk. Tam looked as humiliated as I felt, but Renee's green eyes glittered like something cold and hard—a marble, maybe. Or a glacier.

Mrs. Larsen crossed her arms and sat back in her chair. "I have two identical labs," she said, looking at us, each in turn, "from two different lab tables."

Orren looked at me sharply. I looked at the floor.

"Well . . . we all did the same experiment," Renee hedged.

"Yes," Mrs. Larsen agreed, "but the wording of the labs is exactly the same. Down to the funny title."

"Funny title?" Tam repeated.

I looked up, and Tam's dark eyes stabbed into me.

"One of you, it seems, has a sense of humor," Mrs. Larsen said. "But since I don't know who copied whom, I have to give everyone a zero."

There was a beat of silence while we all let this sink in. A zero. As ten percent of our grade. Now the best any of us could hope for in the class was a B. I could almost feel the grade calculation happening in Orren's mind.

"Mrs. Larsen, isn't there something we can do?" I asked. "Some extra credit?"

"I don't offer extra credit to some students and not others."

"Well, maybe you could give everyone the chance to improve their lab grades," Orren suggested in a voice that was surprisingly calm.

Giving him a sideways look, Mrs. Larsen heaved a sigh.

Oh, please, please, I begged silently. Pleaseplease—pleasepleaseplease. Just let me do this and I will dedicate my life to stamping out cheating—

Finally, Mrs. Larsen pursed her lips, and nodded. "Okay," she said slowly. "Redo the lab by the end of the week, and I'll regrade it. But, in your cases, I'm taking twenty points off for being late," she added. "That means, even if it's perfect, the top grade you can get will be an eighty."

I expected Orren to protest that he hadn't even been involved in the cheating, but instead, he just said, "No problem."

"Thanks, Mrs. Larsen," Renee said.

"Yeah, thanks," I agreed. That was what I liked about Mrs. Larsen—she seemed like a toughie, but she was really just a Milky Way.

"You'd better hurry," the science teacher said. Students were humming past the door out in the hallway. "You'll be late for your next class."

Tam and Renee, who had already grabbed their backpacks, turned and left the room, but Orren and I had to scurry back to our lab table to collect our stuff.

"I'm so sorry," I whispered as I shoved my book into my backpack.

Orren didn't reply. He didn't even look at me.

I don't know why that bugged me. I mean, why should I care if Orren Kendall is mad at me? He's just a total nork who I got stuck with as a lab partner, right?

Right?

Then again, it was totally my fault that he had almost got a zero on a major lab. And I did feel really bad about it. I poked his arm, and he looked up.

"Orren," I said, "I am really sorry."

His green eyes were cloudy. "You gave it to them."

"Yeah," I admitted. "But they really needed it—they were about to get a—"

Okay, at least I had enough of a brain to stop myself before I said, "zero."

"Tam is my best friend," I finished lamely. Isn't she? I wondered. To tell the truth, I wasn't so sure anymore.

Orren pressed his lips together. Then he

hiked his backpack up onto his shoulder, and the anger seemed to drain from him. "It's okay," he said finally. "I probably would have done the same thing."

Suddenly, Orren looked kind of lonely. I felt sad as the meaning of his words hit me. He would have done the same thing . . . if he had any friends. "So, uh, do you want to meet up after school?" I suggested. "To work on the lab?"

Orren hesitated. "I have a soccer game today. So do you."

"Oh, right," I said. I'd completely spaced it. "Okay, how about tomorrow—after practice. Whoever gets out first can meet the other."

"Okay," Orren said hesitantly. Then again, more sure, "Okay."

I glanced at my watch. We were about to be seriously late. "Okay, see you," I said quickly and buzzed out the door.

"Allie!" Tam whispered furiously as I lunged out of the room. She had been waiting for me just outside the door. Grabbing my arm, she dragged me over to the lockers.

Orren glanced at us quickly as he raced out

of the room, but he kept on rolling toward our next class—history. I only had about ten seconds to get there, too. I could hear Tam's apology later. "Hey, look I gotta—"

"What were you thinking, putting a joke title on the lab?" Tam demanded.

I gaped at her, wondering if I'd just misheard. "What?"

"How was I supposed to know the title was a *joke*?" Tam hissed, her eyes flashing dangerously. "Why didn't you tell me that when you gave me the lab? Thanks to your sense of humor, Mrs. Larsen thinks we cheated, and Renee is really mad. God, Allie, why can't you just be normal?"

And then she walked away.

I tried to move, but I couldn't. I was too stunned. I just stood there, stuck in the ground like a streetlamp. Tam was mad—really mad. But this wasn't even my fault—it was hers! Still, I felt afraid. Tam was my best friend. Without her—what did I have? I was just a shadow. A ghost. A nothing walking between classes with no one.

The bell rang, snapping me out of my trance.

Great, I thought, starting to move. Now I'm late.
And Mrs. Gibb made tardy students serve detention during lunch.

This day just kept getting better and better.

---

in•no•sense \'in-no-sens\ *n* : a question that is asked
in an innocent tone of voice, but is really used to
point out that what you're saying makes no sense at all

"Hey, sweetie," Mom said when I walked through
the door later that night. "Good game?" She
was sitting at the kitchen table, flipping through
a recipe book. She does that sometimes—reads
through recipes the way other people read novels.

"It was okay," I admitted as I plopped down
in the chair across from hers. "We won." No
thanks to me, though. Jack had scored the only
goal. I looked down at the recipe Mom was reading, but my eyes barely registered the letters on
the page. "So, uh, did anyone call for me?" I asked
finally.

"Yeah," Mom said, and for a second I got this
hopeful, fluttery feeling in my stomach until she
added, "Dad called."

"Oh."

Mom lifted her eyebrows. I guess I'd sounded more disappointed than I'd meant to. "I mean, *oh!*" I corrected myself.

Mom closed her cookbook and looked at me. I squirmed. "Were you expecting another call?" she prompted.

"Not really," I said quickly.

"Mmm." Mom's gaze didn't shift. "It seems like Tam never calls anymore," she said finally.

"We're kind of in a fight," I admitted. "I think. I'm not exactly sure."

"Have you tried talking to her about it?" Mom asked gently.

"I can't just call her up and say, 'I'm mad at you,'" I snapped. I wasn't even sure why I was annoyed—I knew Mom was only trying to help. It's just that she was sounding a little like Coach Connors: be aggressive, be aggressive. Why do I always have to be the one who does all of the hard stuff? I wondered. "It's not that easy."

Mom nodded like she understood. "So, *not* talking to her is easier?" she asked.

I thought about it for a minute. That's so Mom. She uses this innosense act to make me think. And now I had to confess that she had a point. "I guess not," I admitted. "It's just—it's so hard, you know?"

"Yeah," Mom said gently. "I know."

We were both silent for a while, and I could hear the seconds ticking by on the kitchen clock.

"I'd better call Dad back."

"Homework?" Mom prompted.

"Just a little," I admitted. "Can I call Dad first?"

"Of course," Mom said. She gathered up her books and stashed them away. "I'll be in the other room."

Getting up, I yanked the phone off the wall and punched in Dad's number.

"Hello?"

It was Marci's voice.

"Um, hi, Marci. It's Allie."

"Oh, hi, Allison," Marci said. Stress was giving her voice this tense twang. I could hear Daniel screaming in the background.

"How are you?" I asked. I always get into trouble if I just ask for Dad. I have to go through this charade of talking to Marci first.

"What?" Marci asked as Daniel's wailing grew louder. "I can't hear you."

"How are you?" I repeated, louder.

"Oh, fine," Marci snapped. "Look, I'm sorry but I can't talk now."

"Um . . . okay," I replied. "I was just returning—"

"Do you want to speak to your father?" Marci asked. Then, without waiting for my reply, she said, "Here you go."

"Bye. Good talking with—"

"Hello?" It was Dad. He must have been walking down the hallway, or something, because Daniel's screeching died away in the background.

"Hi, Dad," I said, taking a deep breath. Marci had really freaked me out—it was as if her stress had traveled directly into my ear through the phone wires, or something.

"Hi, Allison. How are things?"

"Ugh," I grunted.

"That bad?" Dad joked. "What happened?"

"Well, Tam and I are kind of in a fight," I admitted.

"I thought she was your best friend," Dad said.

That really bugged me. "She *is* my best friend," I insisted. "It's just—there was kind of this . . . misunderstanding."

"What about?"

I knew I couldn't tell Dad about the cheating, because he'd go Tilt-A-Whirl on me. "Well . . ." I hedged. "We both got bad grades on this science lab."

"How bad?" Dad asked.

"Well . . ." I hedged. "Right now it's a zero."

There was this big, fat, ugly silence until Dad said, "I see."

"But I can bring it up," I offered.

"Well, I hope you're going to do that."

I took a deep breath and thought, does he think I'm a total moron? "Of course I am."

"Because your grades are very important, Allison."

I rolled my eyes. "I know, Dad."

"You need to take this very seriously."

"I do take it seriously."

"Well, I think maybe you should be a little

more concerned about your science grade, and a little less worried about an argument with your friend."

I squeezed the phone tighter, regretting that I'd even brought it up. Once my dad gets something like this in his head, there's no getting it out. I mean, how could I make him understand that the grade was something I could fix, but that my friendship with Tam . . . well, I wasn't so sure? "Okay, Dad," I said finally. "Listen, I have to go do my homework, okay?"

"Isn't it a little late to be starting your homework?"

Grr! "I just have to finish up a few things. Give Daniel a kiss for me, okay?"

"All right, Allison. Let me know what happens in science."

"Okay. Night, Dad. Love you."

"Good night."

Sighing, I hung up. That conversation had stunk. I should have known better than to try to tell him about Tam. I really don't understand how Mom can seem to get the whole thing without my saying a word, while Dad doesn't get it no matter how much I explain. I'll call him again after Mrs. Larsen regrades my lab, I decided. I grabbed my backpack and headed for the stairs.

Hey. At least my social studies textbook wasn't going to get on my back about my grades or about being my best friend. And I was pretty sure I could beat it at soccer.

That was something, right?

smile•ci•cle \'smile-si-kel \ *n* : a totally fake smile that gets frozen to your face and makes your cheek muscles hurt

I felt like a donkey, or some other pack animal, weighed down by my backpack and a sack full of clothes and soccer cleats as I made my way toward the boys' practice fields. I was still wearing my grass-stained practice clothes, but I had changed into normal sneakers.

As I rounded the rear of the science building, I saw that the guys were still out on the field, so I quickened my pace. Please please please, I begged silently, please don't let practice end before I get there. I scurried toward the fields while still trying to look as cool and nonchalant as possible.

I had been praying all through soccer practice that we would get out a little early so that I could meet Orren at the boys' fields. That way, I'd get to see Chris running around in his soccer shorts. I squinted, and found him right away——he had the ball and was racing toward the goal.

A clammy chill passed over my body, and I felt like I'd stepped into a giant blob of Jell-O, or something. I caught my breath.

Cutting right, Chris took the shot. *Slam!* A rocket.

But not good enough. The goalie grabbed the ball as easily as if he were picking an orange off a tree. Man, I thought, nice hands.

Hey, I realized with a smile as the goalie kicked the ball back into play. That's Justin. I watched the ball bounce among the group of guys on the field, and I was amazed at how many of them I knew. Orren was out there, too. I smiled.

Orren had completely saved me in science class today. He'd been so intense about making sure that we both knew where and when to meet after school and what to bring that I barely had a chance to glance at Tam before class or after. Which was just as well. She'd spent the whole day ignoring me.

Hearing a giggle, I turned and saw two

girls sitting on the bottom step of the nearby bleachers. Curly black hair and glossy blond. Tam and Renee.

Suddenly, the blob of Jell-O that had held me rooted to my spot staring at Chris dissolved into a gooey, sticky mess. I felt nauseated.

This is kind of sick, but I'd actually been kind of glad that Mrs. Gibb had given me detention for being late the day before. That way, I could sit out lunch period in her classroom, rather than having to face Tam.

I guess I could have asked Jack if I could sit at her table, but I still felt kind of dumb doing that. I mean, it was one thing if she wanted to invite me. But I didn't want to look like some friendless loser in front of Chris.

I'd much rather look like a loser in detention.

But I couldn't let this go on forever. Tam and I had to make up eventually. Maybe I should try to talk to her, like Mom had said. . . .

I hesitated for another thirty seconds before I finally plastered a smilecicle on my face and decided to go over there.

"Hey, Tam," I said, climbing up the bleachers and sitting on the seat behind her. "Hey, Renee."

"Hi, Allie." Tam's voice was an empty puff, like a jelly doughnut with no jelly.

"Love your outfit," Renee said with this little smirk. Tam giggled.

"Oh, yeah," I said, blushing as I looked down at my dirty shorts and T-shirt. That's what I hate about Renee. She never says anything like, *You smell like a hairy armpit*, or *You're as ugly as a dinosaur's butt*, she just makes some kind of little comment so that you can't tell whether she likes you and is teasing you, or whether she hates your guts and is mocking you. And if you get all bent out of shape, she'll be like, "Chill out, I was just joking!"

"Are you here to see your boyfriend?" Renee asked.

Tam flashed her a warning look, and I was glad that she was finally annoyed by Renee. "Orren isn't my boyfriend. We're just going to the library to fix our lab."

"I wasn't talking about Orren," Renee shot back, giving her blond hair a toss. "I was talking about Chris." She smiled, but only with one side of her mouth. "I can't believe you still like him, Allie. Do you still have your collection of little plastic horses, too?"

For a minute, I could feel the earth spinning in space. I opened my mouth to deny that I liked Chris, but it was too late—my face was red-hot. How did she know? I wondered. How could she have figured it out?

But the answer was staring me in the face. Tam had told her.

"It's funny that you still like him, Allie," Renee went on. "Because I don't think you're really his . . . type."

My face was burning so brightly that, looking back on it, I'm amazed that the people around me didn't end up with a nice tan. My eyes started to fill up, which only embarrassed me more. I couldn't believe I was almost crying because Renee knew about my crush. But it wasn't just that. I mean, okay, my crush on Chris was kind of hopeless. But it really hurt my feelings to think that Tam thought so, too—and that she and Renee had been laughing about it behind my back.

Just then, the coach's whistle blew, and I hauled myself off the bleacher seat. I had never been so grateful to be heading to the library in my life.

"Allie—" Tam called, but I didn't turn around.

———

go **Mup•pet** \'go 'mup-et\ *v* : to flail the arms wildly and let out a high-pitched scream, much like Kermit the Frog, Elmo, or Grover when they are spazzing out

"So how about, 'Acids Rock, Bases Rule'?" I suggested in my best library whisper. We had been working on our lab for about an hour, and we were almost done. A problem with Orren was that sometimes he kind of spaced out, and I had to repeat myself. Normally, that wouldn't have annoyed me, but I was still in a horrible mood over the Tamara thing. "Or we could go with, 'Covering the Bases.' Or maybe we shouldn't try to be funny at all. . . ."

Orren didn't reply. He was flipping through our textbook, trying to find more information on how pH was calculated.

I blew out an exasperated breath. "Your silence is very encouraging."

He still didn't say anything. I sighed, wondering whether his anger over our lab had finally kicked in. "Orren," I said. "Orren!"

Orren finally looked up. "Hmm? What? Were you saying something?"

The librarian looked over at us and frowned. Orren seemed to have forgotten he was in the library, and his voice was kind of loud.

I motioned for him to keep it down. "Are you okay?" I whispered. "You seem kind of out of it."

"Sorry." Orren shook his head. He sighed. "It's just that this is the first F I've ever gotten."

"On anything?"

Orren nodded.

I gaped at him. He'd never got an F. It didn't seem right. "You mean you've never flunked a pop quiz, or a homework assignment, or anything?"

Orren stared down at his textbook. "My parents freak out about my grades."

"Yeah . . . my dad is kind of like that."

"Really?" Orren looked surprised.

"But my mom always says that as long as I do my best, that's what's important."

"Nice mom."

"Yeah."

We sat in silence for a moment.

"You know the funny thing about getting this zero?" Orren asked suddenly, as though the thought had just occurred to him. "It really . . . it really wasn't that bad."

I smiled. "Don't get too used to it."

"Don't worry." Orren laughed, like the very thought was ridiculous. "It's just . . . I guess I thought my parents would totally lose it. But they didn't. I mean, they weren't happy. But they were okay."

I was actually kind of glad that Orren had told me about his parents. It sort of explained why he acted like the fate of the universe hung on each of our homework assignments, and why he would hiss "Yess!" and pump his fist every time he got a hundred on a quiz. It's amazing that you can sit right next to someone, and not ever really know what's going on in their brain.

Just then, a pair of hands covered my eyes, and someone with a fake French accent said, "Now you muz' guess 'oo eet ees."

"Pepe le Pew?" I suggested.

There were a few laughs, and someone said, "Close. Good guess."

That voice I knew. Jack. Which meant that the French voice had to be—"Elena."

"Jack, you gave it away," Elena griped as she pulled her hands away, then plopped into the seat next to mine. She grinned at Orren. "I'm Elena."

"Orren," he said.

"Orren, this is Jack," I said as she took the chair next to him.

"You play soccer with my cousin," Jack said.

"Yeah." Orren looked like he was shocked that she had noticed. "I see you after practice sometimes."

"What are you guys doing here?" I asked.

"Elena was over at my house," Jack explained. "Mom's dropping her off, but we're here to pick up Chris, since it's on the way."

"Speaking of . . ." Elena said, looking behind me.

I turned just in time to see Chris coming down the spiral staircase that led to the nonfiction section on the second floor. He smiled when he saw us. "Hey! It's the welcome wagon!"

"Minus the wagon," Elena joked.

I snuck a look at Chris. Jack was saying something, and his big blue eyes were fastened on her. He needed a haircut—one curl looped around the side of his ear, curling around his earlobe.

"—so are you, Allie?"

I snapped back to reality just in time to realize that everyone was looking at me. Jack had just asked me a question. "Uh, sorry," I admitted. "I was kind of on another planet for a minute. What?"

"I was just asking if we were all going to the sports banquet?" Jack repeated. "Coach Connors mentioned it at the end of practice."

"Oh, uh, sure," I said.

"I'll be there," Chris said, and my heart lurched like Frankenstein's monster. Thank God I said I'd be there! I thought. Maybe we'll all sit together!

"Okay, well, my mom's waiting, so we'd

better jet," Jack said. "See you later, Allie. Good meeting you, Orren."

"Bye," I said as Orren waved. I watched them leave for a minute. Well, I watched *Chris* leave. I couldn't tear my eyes away until the door closed behind him.

When I turned back, I saw that Orren was smirking at me.

I frowned. "What are you grinning at?"

He shrugged. "Nothing." He started flipping slowly through his science book, but he was still grinning.

I slapped my hand in the middle of his book so that he couldn't flip anymore. I waited until he looked up before I growled, "What?"

Orren lifted his eyebrows and sat back in his chair. "Someone has a crush," he said in this self-satisfied way.

He was so smug that it made me want to go Muppet on him. But I remained in control. "I don't know what you're talking about."

Orren leaned forward in his chair. "Look me in the eye and tell me that you don't like Chris."

I opened my mouth, but it was hopeless. "I hate you," I told him. "How could you tell?"

Orren shrugged. "Your eyes weren't following the conversation." He chuckled in this *I'm so smart* kind of way. Why did I have to get Sherlock Holmes as a lab partner? I wondered.

"Please don't tell."

"I never would," he said, all indignant, like the mere suggestion was an insult. "It's just funny . . . Chris doesn't really seem like your type."

I rolled my eyes, demanding, "Why does everyone keep saying that?"

"I have no idea," Orren admitted. "I don't even know what that means. But you just seem like you'd be weird together."

"I guess it's pretty hopeless," I admitted with a sigh.

"I didn't mean that—" Orren said, then stopped. "I don't know what I mean."

Silence settled over us.

"Okay," I said after a moment. "Let's finish the lab." I turned to our work, but a little worry mouse still gnawed at my heart. I looked Orren in the eye. "Promise you won't tell?"

"I promise," Orren repeated. His face was completely serious.

And for some reason, I believed him. It was really kind of depressing to think that I could trust Orren to keep a secret more than I could trust my own best friend.

pup•pet mas•ter \'puh•pet 'mas•ter\ *n* : someone who pulls all the strings and sometimes likes to jerk you around

"Mom!" I shouted as I walked in the back door. "I'm h—"

"I'm right here, Allie," Mom said, and that was when I saw that she was sitting at the kitchen table . . . with Tam. Tam had a plate with half a brownie on it, and I was struck by how normal that seemed, and then I was struck by how weird it was that it should seem normal, because Tam hadn't been over to my house in weeks. She used to come over and hang out all the time . . . but that was last summer, last year. Not this year. Not since sixth grade.

"Hi, Allie," Tam said.

I dropped my backpack on the floor. "Hey."

There was this crushing silence, and Mom looked from my face to Tam's and then back again. "Well," she said finally, "Allie, I'll be upstairs if you need me. Tam, it was great seeing you. Don't be such a stranger."

I was struck with this urge to say, *Yeah, Tam, don't be such a stranger.* But I just couldn't say it. I may have to be a striker on the soccer field, I thought, but I don't feel like striking right now.

Then Mom walked out of the room and we were alone.

I just stood there, leaning against the countertop, looking at Tam. I wasn't about to be the first one to speak. Mostly because I had no idea what I wanted to say.

"So," Tam said awkwardly, "did you get your lab done?"

"Yeah," I snapped. You did not come over here to ask to copy my lab, I thought, completely furious. If that's why you came over—

"Yeah, us too." Tam nodded, and looked back at her brownie. "It wasn't really that hard."

The adrenaline that had been pumping through my body left me feeling loose-limbed and light-headed. Well, at least she isn't here to cheat off my homework. "So—what are you doing here?" I asked.

Tam waited for a second. "Look, I'm sorry . . . about Renee."

Sorry that she's a complete witch? I thought. "What about her?"

"Just . . . she wasn't supposed to say anything," Tam said, her black eyes pleading. "I didn't mean to tell her about Chris, it just . . . slipped out."

"Is she going to go tell the whole school now?"

Tam shook her head. "I made her promise not to. She won't. I swear."

My chest felt tight. "She didn't have to be so mean about it," I said finally.

"She was just joking." Tam's voice was defensive.

Why are you letting Renee be your puppet master? I thought. But what I said was, "I didn't think it was funny."

Tam's eyes flashed darkly. "Well, she didn't mean anything by it," she insisted. "Besides, she has a point. You and Chris are kind of—"

I glared at her. "Kind of what?"

"It's just . . . he was never really more than a

dream, Allie," Tam said in this quiet voice, almost like she felt sorry for me. "Like having a crush on a movie star."

I knew what Tam was saying, but I thought she was wrong. Sure, Chris was older, but he *wasn't* a movie star. He was just a guy in our school. And he was someone that I hung out with . . . you know . . . sometimes. Kind of.

"I'm sorry." And Tam really did look sorry.

But that didn't make me feel any better.

Just to make the moment extra special, Lionel chose that second to walk into the kitchen. "Hey, Tamara," he said, stopping in his tracks when he saw her. "Long time no see." Turning quickly, I yanked open the fridge and peered inside so that he wouldn't see my eyes. Blinking hard, I grabbed the OJ, then kept my back to Lionel as I got a glass from the cupboard.

"Hey, Lionel," Tam replied. "What's new?"

"Not much. Ooh, look, Allie's actually using a glass," Lionel cracked. "Tam, have you been teaching Allie how to act normal?"

"Trying to," Tam said, and I swear, at that moment, I wanted to punch her, or scream, or burst out crying. Anything. Anything would be better than this silent war, where everything had two meanings, and nobody said what they thought. Tam got up from her chair. "I've got to get home. Allie, I'll talk to you later?"

"Sure," I said.

Then Tam gave me a little wave as she walked out the back door, which closed with a slam. I put my empty juice glass in the sink.

Lionel looked at me carefully. "Are you okay?" Lionel asked. I must have looked pretty upset, because Lionel actually sounded worried.

"Fine," I croaked. But that was a lie.

I staggered out of the kitchen and upstairs to my room, fuming. Tam had waved good-bye with her right hand. She was wearing a ring, but it wasn't our friendship ring. I realized with a pang that I hadn't seen her wear it in weeks. It was as though it had disappeared.

Why? I wondered. Why? Okay, maybe I didn't dress as well as Renee, even with my new clothes, and maybe I wasn't into shopping and all that junk. But I'd never been into that stuff. I wasn't the one who had changed.

What is her problem? I thought as I flung my bag at the foot of my bed. We were friends. Best friends! She couldn't just treat me like some loser.

It was like what she was saying about Chris. Was it really so impossible to believe that he could ever be interested in me? Okay, sure, he was a golden god, and I was a . . . well, a sort of spazzy sixth grader. But he was also a plain old guy.

I need to show Tam that she's completely wrong about me, I realized. And suddenly, I had an idea. I would ask Chris to the sports banquet. I'd ask him, and he'd say yes, and then Tam would see that Renee was an idiot, and that she had me all wrong.

Peebles strutted into my room as I flopped onto my bed. "All I have to do is ask him." My cat jumped up next to me and she craned her neck to butt my hand with her head. "I mean, it's not like he's going to say no, right?"

Peebles blinked at me, and I scratched behind her ears. Purring, she stepped up onto my belly, poking me in the stomach with her little cat feet as she turned around three times and then lay down.

It's a start, I thought as I patted Peebles on the head. At least somebody believes in me.

---

par•o•lies \ pa-'rol-eez \ *n* **1:** kids from parochial school **2:** uptight preps with no sweat glands **3:** girls whose hair stays perfectly braided, even while playing contact sports

"Get aggressive!" Coach Connors shouted as I flipped the ball to Jack for about the twentieth time that day. "You've got to take those shots, Allie!"

Why doesn't she just make a CD of one day's worth of shouting? I wondered as the other team's goalie—a tiny girl who reminded me of a jumping flea—blocked a tremendous shot and kicked the ball back into play. Coach always repeated herself with me: "Get aggressive! Get aggressive!" When was she going to figure out that I didn't *want* to get aggressive—that I wanted to do what I already knew how to do?

The other team tried a shot, and Elena headed it away from our goal just in time. The ball whizzed past my face. Luckily, Jack was all over it. She dribbled the ball downfield, toward the flea. I sprinted after her.

Jack was getting a lot of pressure from this blond French-braid girl defending her. We were playing the girls from Saint Agnes, and they were a lot tougher than they looked. You know the type: glossy hair, painted fingernails, and tiny gold hoop earrings. In a soccer game! When they jogged out onto the field in their superclean, fabric-softener-scented uniforms, I'd thought, See ya later, parolies.

Well, guess what? Saint Agnes must have been the patron saint of soccer, because these girls were kicking our butts. It was the second half, and we were down by two. It didn't look like we were getting anything past the flea.

I cut a hard right and ditched the lip-gloss queen who was defending me. In a flash, Jack snapped me the ball.

"Go for it, Allie!" Coach screamed.

Stop yelling at me! I thought. Gritting my teeth, I lined up my shot. Top corner. It was an impossible angle, but I had to try it.

Suddenly, I felt someone looking at me. After weeks of finely tuning my Chris compass, it was like I had some freakish sixth sense that told me when he was nearby. Like now. Top of the bleachers, next to Justin. They were watching the game.

Ignore him! I thought as I took the shot. It was gorgeous, just where I wanted it . . . but no goal. That stupid flea jumped higher than humanly possible and nabbed the ball just before it went in.

"Allie, look alive!" Coach called from the sidelines.

Argh! I chased after the ball, pouring on the speed, but the other team had intercepted it, and I had to cut fast back toward our goal.

When did Chris get here? I wondered as I zoomed upfield. Could he possibly have been here for the whole game? Would he be here after? Maybe I could ask him then. *Chris, I was wondering whether you were going to the sports banquet,* I rehearsed as I chased after the ball. A quick pass across the field, and I had to stumble off in another direction. Because I'm going, I thought, and so, like, maybe we could go together. . . .

My heart was throbbing with the effort of the game, and with the fear of asking Chris to the banquet. My knees felt like they were made of Silly Putty. I guess that was how the other team managed to kick the ball right through them.

Tell me he didn't see that! I thought. Okay, that last move actually made me mad. I lunged after the ball and went after it like it was a sack of cash. A girl with a slick brown ponytail slammed a serious kick into my shin guard, but it didn't even phase me. I knocked the ball toward Elena, and took off toward Saint Agnes's goal.

Elena was all over it. With a quick pass, Jack had the ball, then Sally, and soon it was all the way at the other end of the field. Suddenly, the ball was headed right for me.

Don't miss, don't miss! I thought as I dribbled toward the goal. I had the shot, but suddenly, I didn't dare take it. What if I missed again in front of Chris? I'd die. I'd die, and I wouldn't be able to ask him to the sports banquet because I'd be dead. Before I even realized I'd made a decision, I'd given the ball a sideways slam to Jack, who thundered it into the goal. But it wasn't enough.

Five minutes later, the game was over. We'd lost.

I trudged over to our bench and stood there like a lump as everyone gathered around to give the old, "Who do we appreciate?" cheer. I hate that stupid cheer. They should just make it "We like fruits and we like nuts—thanks for kicking all our butts!" or something. Oh, yeah—I really *appreciated* getting creamed.

Anyway, so we gave our cheer, and Saint Agnes gave their cheer, and that was the end. I started shoving stuff into my bag. I was antsy— I wanted to find Chris and ask him to the banquet as soon as possible. All of a sudden, I felt this shadow fall across my face. I looked up, and saw Coach standing over me, the setting sun fading red behind her head. With the ball in her hand, she looked like the living incarnation of Agnes, Soccer Saint.

"That shot you took was a tough one," Coach Connors said. "Good effort."

"Not good enough," I said, yanking at my shoelace.

"No." Coach's voice was so sharp that I looked up into her serious face. "It *was* good enough. You tried. That takes courage. That's all

I'm asking for." She looked at me for a moment more, and then she walked away.

I blinked as I watched her retreating into the swirl of soccer players. What is she saying? I wondered. That she doesn't care about winning? I didn't believe it for a minute.

"Rough game, huh?" Jack flopped onto the bench beside me and started untying her cleats.

I shook my head. "The girl defending me didn't even smudge her lip gloss. I mean, I can't even put lip gloss *on* without smudging it!"

"What's the deal with those girls?" Elena griped as she trudged over and flopped on the grass near us. She was still breathing hard, and the back of her jersey was soaked. "They weren't even sweating! They all walked off the field smelling like springtime!"

"So," Jack said, "who's coming out to celebrate?"

I snorted. "We lost!"

Jack shrugged. "So what?"

"You need a celebration *more* after you've lost," Elena pointed out.

I had to admit, this was a good point.

"Everyone goes," Jack agreed, giving me a little nudge. "The M&M's take us, then drop us off at home afterward."

I smiled. The M&M's is an expression I had come up with. It stands for Moms and Minivans. For some reason, it made me really happy that Jack had just used it.

"I'll have to call my mom," I hedged.

"You can call from the restaurant," Jack said. "All the moms have cell phones."

I nodded, but I was hardly paying attention—I was too busy scanning the crowd. Where is Chris? I wondered. I couldn't see him.

Suddenly, I felt a hand on my shoulder. I'd been so focused on looking for Chris that I nearly jumped out of my skin.

"Oh, Orren!" My lab partner was smiling down at me, but my heart sank. I didn't have time to chat—I needed to find Chris.

"Great game," Orren said warmly. "Saw your steal."

"Oh . . . thanks. Too bad we lost." I shouldered my bag and stood up, hoping that was all he wanted to say. Could I just walk off? I wondered, but that seemed kind of rude.

"Allie, can I talk to you for a minute?" Orren asked.

I scanned the crowd again, but there was still no sign of Chris. Had he left already? That would be just my luck—for Chris to have only seen the part of the game in which I totally stank. "What's up?" I asked Orren absently.

Orren cleared his throat. "Well, I ran into Mrs. Larsen after school. She regraded our lab, and we're getting an eighty on it, so that's good."

"Oh!" I said brightly. "Oh, great. Thanks for letting me know." I started to walk off, but Orren didn't move, so I sort of stumbled and took another awkward step back toward him. "Is there something else?"

"Uh . . . yeah," Orren said slowly.

I waited.

"I . . . uh . . . was wondering if you were going to the sports banquet," he said.

A cold fist squeezed my heart. "Yeah," I said faintly. Please don't do what I think you're going to do, I thought desperately. Please don't—

"Oh. Great. Because I'm going, too. And I thought that we could go together. . . ."

Like invisible arrows, the words flew through the air and shot through my chest. It was almost as though they had pinned me against something. I couldn't move. I couldn't breathe.

Orren was staring at me in that intense way he has. I felt almost as though his green eyes were peeling back the layers of skin, probing into my brain.

I didn't know what to say. Yes? No? I didn't want to go with Orren. I wanted to go with Chris. But if I said no, would Orren think it was because I thought he was a nerd? If I said yes, would I just be doing it because I felt sorry for him? *Did* I feel sorry for Orren? Was I one of those jerks who judge people on superficial stuff? I wondered. Or was I just the kind of idiot who does the nice things because they're too dumb to say no?

And now Renee was going to see me with Orren instead of with Chris. I could just imagine what she would have to say about it.

The thoughts flashed by like cars at the Indy 500. *Zip! Zip! Zip!* Then they were gone, and I was left in the moment, standing there, facing Orren.

"Sure!" I heard myself say in this freakishly chipper voice. "Sounds great!"

"Okay," Orren said, and this huge smile washed over his face. He looked so relieved that I felt like I'd been stabbed with another arrow. "Okay, great. Well, have fun getting ice cream. I'll see you tomorrow."

I nodded and gave him a smile. I couldn't speak. My throat had completely closed, and I wondered whether "Sounds great!" would be the last thing that I'd ever be able to say for the rest of my life.

Orren trotted off, and I took a huge breath and turned to face the empty soccer field, tears streaming down my face. I just stood there, crying. I wasn't even sure why.

"Hey, Allie, wake up! Ice cream time!" Elena skipped over to me and wrapped an arm around my shoulder. But her smile evaporated when she saw my face. "Oh my god," she said quickly, her eyes growing wide, "what's wrong?"

Jack was with her, and her eyebrows drew together as she looked at me.

"It's nothing," I said, wiping my face quickly. I pivoted slightly, so that I wasn't facing the team. "It's stupid."

Jack and Elena continued to stand there, looking so worried that I had to laugh. I knew that I was just making a big deal out of nothing; but that thought just made another stream of tears pour down my face. "No, *really*, it's stupid," I told them. "You won't believe how stupid it is."

"Try us," Jack urged.

"Did Orren say something to you?" Elena demanded. She looked like she was ready to rip his head off and kick it into the soccer net.

"No, no," I told her quickly. "Well, yes, but nothing bad." I took a deep breath. "It's just, he asked me to go with him to the sports banquet." And then the waterworks started again.

"Well, that isn't so bad, is it?" Elena asked gently.

"No." I shook my head and took a shaky breath. "It's just that . . . I kind of wanted to go with someone else." I pressed my lips together and swallowed hard. "I was kind of planning on asking that person today."

"That's hard," Jack said sympathetically. "But look, Allie, Orren is probably just asking as a friend. I'm sure he isn't thinking of this as some big romance."

Ohmygosh, it hadn't even occurred to me that Orren might think that this was some big romance! What if he thinks I said yes because I like him? I thought desperately. What if he has a crush on me? Groaning, I rubbed my temples.

"Why don't you just back out?" Jack suggested.

"But I really do want to go to the banquet," I said.

"Then tell him that you just don't want to go with him," Elena said.

I shook my head. "I could never do that."

"Yeah," Jack said with a sigh, "me neither."

"Unless I totally hated the guy," Elena volunteered.

And I don't hate Orren, I thought. I took a deep breath. "Okay," I said finally. "I'm okay. This is no big deal."

"Right." Elena nodded. "Nothing that a little ice cream can't solve."

"Besides, we'll all be there," Jack added. "No big."

"Yeah, no big." I smiled, and it was a real smile, not one of those shaky, propped-up fake smiles. "Thanks, guys."

Jack and Elena were right. This was no big deal. Okay, so I wasn't going to the banquet with Chris. But at least it wasn't because he'd said no. That would really be something to cry about.

"Okay, now it's *really* ice cream time," Elena said. She wrapped her arm around my shoulder, and Jack wrapped her arm around my other shoulder, and we walked toward the waiting mini-vans just like that—locked in a three-way hug.

- 10 -

road chick•en \'rode 'chi-ken\ *n* : someone who can't decide which side to be on, and ends up standing in the middle of the road . . . which is, of course, where the cars are

When I got home, there was this low buzzing sound coming from the bathroom. The door was slightly open, so I peeked inside. Lionel had spread newspapers all over the sink. The newspaper was covered with clumps of reddish hair. Lionel was using the ancient hair clipper that Mom had used to give Lionel buzz cuts before he announced he never wanted a haircut again.

"What are you doing?" I asked.

Lionel looked up at me and rolled his eyes. "What does it look like I'm doing?" he asked. He surveyed his head in the mirror, then jabbed the clipper at the right side of his head. There was a loud hum and a crackle as another clump of hair fell softly onto the paper, like an auburn snowflake. He nodded, apparently satisfied, and pulled the long guide off the end of the hair clipper.

"I mean, I *see* what you're doing," I explained, "but I don't see why. I thought you liked having long hair."

"It was okay, but I got kind of sick of it," Lionel said. "Besides, we're going out to dinner with Dad tonight, remember?"

"Oh." Right. Dad *hates* Lionel's shaggy hair. When we saw Dad at the beginning of the summer, he wouldn't shut up about it. He kept saying that Lionel looked like a girl. Finally, Lionel gave in and let Dad take him for a haircut. But he'd been growing it out since then. "Well, it looks good."

"Yeah?" Lionel looked surprised.

I shrugged. "Yeah." Lionel's hair didn't look that bad—he'd done a pretty good job. I'd gotten so used to seeing him with long, shaggy hair that I'd kind of forgotten what his face looked like. It was thinner than I remembered. Actually, Lionel looked kind of grown up.

Lionel looked at himself in the mirror, and then smiled at me. "Thanks," he said. "I was a little worried about it. I should have asked Mom to take me for a haircut, but I didn't make up my mind until just now, and then there wasn't time, so . . ."

Wow, I thought. Here we are, having a normal conversation. I'd kind of forgotten that it was possible to talk to Lionel.

"Anyway, it'll make Dad happy. And *she* won't be at dinner," Lionel went on, meaning Marci. We feel pretty much the same about her. "So I won't have to hear about how I should have had a professional do it."

"Yeah, and we won't have to get a lecture on table manners," I agreed.

Lionel laughed. Marci always acted like Lionel and I were total slobs. Which was really funny, considering that she had a three-year-old who was usually covered in mysterious goo, and was nearly always pitching fits, demanding more cookies and/or large amounts of ice cream. Don't get me wrong. I love Daniel. I just don't love the way Marci pretends that she's the perfect mom, while our mom is raising wild beasts.

Lionel shook his head and started to pack up the clipper. It was weird—suddenly, I was kind of grateful for my brother. It was a relief to know that someone else felt the same way about our stepmother—that it wasn't just all my imagination. You know, I never felt that I could talk to Mom about Marci, because she clearly makes Mom uncomfortable. And nobody else really knows what Marci is like. But Lionel does.

"You know, you missed a spot," I told Lionel.

Lionel frowned at the mirror. "Where?"

"The back." I tugged at a long tuft that was sticking out behind his left ear. "Want me to get it?"

"Sure." Lionel handed me the clipper, and I flipped it on. It buzzed in my hand as I focused on the spot.

Buzz.

"Oh my God," I said, jumping away from Lionel's head as a huge chunk of hair fell onto the newspaper.

His eyes were huge. "What did you do?"

"I'm sorry—" I said, staring at the stripe of white scalp behind Lionel's ear.

Lionel gaped down at the clipper. We had forgotten to put the guide back on.

"What did you do?" Lionel's voice was a shriek.

"Sorry! Sorry! Lionel, I'm so sorry!" I really meant it, too . . . but as I stared at that bald chunk on his head . . . I just couldn't help it. I started giggling.

"I'm going to kill you!" Lionel grabbed the clipper from my hand and lunged at my head. I screamed.

"What's going on in—oh my God, Lionel, what happened?" The look on Mom's face when she saw Lionel's hair was so funny that I started to giggle again.

"Allie did it." He glared at me.

"I didn't mean to," I pleaded. "I didn't know the guide was off. . . ." My voice faltered and my laughter dried up as Lionel's eyes filled with tears.

"We have to go out with Dad tonight," Lionel said.

"I know, sweetheart," Mom said, giving him a hug. "It's okay. We can fix it. It's not a big deal."

"It *is* a big deal." Lionel's eyes sliced through me like laser beams. "Don't fall asleep," he warned.

"Okay, that's enough," Mom said. "Allie, I

think you'd better let me handle this, okay?" She gave me a *Please get out of here* look, so I just nodded and stepped out of the bathroom, closing the door behind me.

My phone rang the minute I walked into my room.

"Allie?"

"Tam," I said warmly, thrilled that I could tell her the Lionel hair story. "You'll never guess what just—"

"Did Sir Dorksalot ask you to the banquet?"

The receiver turned to ice in my hand. I pressed my lips together, silently cursing myself. For a moment, I'd actually forgotten that Tam and I weren't really friends right now. It took me a minute to switch gears. "What?"

"I heard that Orren asked you to be his date to the sports banquet. And that you said yes. Is that true?"

"How did you hear about that?"

"Who *cares*? Is it true?"

"Well . . . we're just going as friends. . . ."

Silence.

"You can't go."

She said it just like that—like she was a judge, and that was my sentence.

"What?"

"Allie, you can't go to the banquet with him. I mean, you don't want to, do you?"

I couldn't lie. "Well, no . . ."

"Thank God. I thought you were losing your mind for a minute."

"But I can't just cancel—"

Tam blew an exasperated sigh into the receiver. "Allie, you're too nice. Believe me— you're going to regret it. The whole school is going to think that Orren is your boyfriend!"

"But I don't want to hurt his feelings."

"Why do you even care about his feelings? You don't even like him! You'll give him the wrong impression if you go with him."

I heard what she was saying. By telling Orren yes, but not really meaning it, I was definitely being a road chicken. I didn't want Orren to think that we were dating, or anything. And I didn't want anyone else to think that, either. But I also heard what she *wasn't* saying. She didn't want me to go with Orren because it would make her look bad. She didn't want to deal with him. She didn't want to be seen hanging out with him.

"Look, I've got to go," Tam said. "Either way, you're going to ruin someone's night. Ruin Orren's by canceling, or ruin your own, by going with him."

"Okay, Tam," I said finally. "I'll think about it."

"Good. Look, I'll see you tomorrow morning, and we'll figure out something you can say to him that won't hurt his feelings too badly."

I sighed, wondering what that could possibly be. Clicking the OFF button, I went and sat in my window seat. Two doors down, I could see Justin kicking around a soccer ball in his backyard. He dribbled it back and forth, back and forth, cutting away from imaginary opponents, scoring imaginary goals. He was scowling at the ball, like it had insulted his mom or something, and I got the sense that he was enjoying kicking it around. Actually, that looked like a pretty good idea.

Almost without thinking, I found myself heading down the stairs and out the back door and shouting, "Justin!"

Looking up in surprise, Justin gave me a grin

and kicked the ball clear into my yard. Then he jumped our chain-link fence, scaling it with a metallic clatter.

"Hey," he said, dropping lightly into my backyard.

"You're Justin Thyme," I told him. "I'm really in the mood to kick something."

"I hope you're talking about the ball, and not about me," Justin joked.

I grinned. "Either one."

Justin kicked the ball to me, and we knocked it back and forth a little, not seriously. "So what's wrong?" Justin asked.

"Ahh . . ." I shrugged. "This guy asked me to go the sports banquet with him, and I said yes, even though I kind of don't want to go with him."

"Orren?" Justin asked. "I thought you guys were friends."

"How do you know about it?" I demanded. I wasn't used to being talked about. "God, does everybody know?"

"Tam told me," Justin admitted. "I ran into her after soccer. But she thought you'd back out."

"She did?" At this point, I don't know why that news shocked me.

"Will you?" Justin asked.

"I have no idea," I told him honestly.

Justin shrugged. "Orren's a cool guy."

I laughed. "You're the only one who thinks so."

"Well, he's a *nerd*," Justin admitted. "But he's cool. He's a cool nerd."

"He's a pecooliar dude," I said, half to myself.

Justin laughed. "Pecooliar," he repeated. "I like that. And I think you're cool for not automatically turning him down. Most girls would have."

I sighed. "Tam really thinks I shouldn't go with him."

"It's not a big deal, Allie." Justin knocked the ball my way. "You're friends. Right?"

"Yeah, you know that. And I know it. . . ."

"I'm sure Orren knows it, too."

I didn't feel like explaining that it wasn't Orren I was worried about.

It was everyone else.

flie \'fly\ *n* : a little, tiny lie, one that really hardly counts

I stared into my closet, frowning at my options. This is the problem with going out to dinner with Dad—he always wants me to wear a skirt. But the last time I'd worn a skirt I felt like a Dweebosaurus and had the worst day ever. Besides, it was a Tuesday night. I had on jeans, and I didn't particularly feel like changing. I'd already had to get dressed for school, then dressed for soccer, then redressed after soccer, and I didn't want to get undressed and dressed again.

Then again, I really didn't want to hear a lecture on how I should dress more "femininely." It's funny, my dad is proud of the fact that I play soccer, but he basically wants me to be this very girly athlete. You know, like those Saint Agnes girls. That's how Marci is. She likes to jog. But she gets more dressed up for her daily run than I do when I'm going to church. She even wears *makeup*.

Sighing, I hauled my red plaid pants from the closet, figuring on a compromise. They were sort of funky, but dressier than jeans. I paired them with this cool black long-sleeved shirt with red Chinese characters on it, and my chunky black boots, then looked in the mirror. Not bad. But my hair was doing this annoying frizz thing, so I twisted the front backward into little snakes on either side of my face and clipped them with small sparkly minibarrettes. Then I dug this ancient lip gloss out of my drawer and smeared some over my lips. Unbelievably, it actually ended up looking pretty good. Wow, I thought as I smiled at myself in the mirror. Maybe I'm getting the hang of this. I mean, I was still no Tam or Renee—I was just a really good version of me.

I heard gravel crunch in our driveway, and I was halfway down the stairs by the time the doorbell rang.

"Dad!" I shouted as I flung open the door.

"Allison!" Dad grinned and gave me a hug. "How's middle-school life treating my prettiest girl?"

I shut the door as Dad stepped into the hall. "Eh," I said.

"That good, huh?" His green eyes were laughing.

I smiled up at him. I don't know why, but I'm always surprised whenever I see my dad. He always looks younger than I remember him. He used to be in the marines, and he's still in really good shape. He almost always wears a suit, except on the weekends, when he wears khaki pants or khaki shorts (ironed) and a polo shirt (also ironed). I don't know if I've ever seen him in jeans, except for this one time that we went horseback riding—and the jeans he wore had creases down the front. He always wears his hair in a crew cut. When I looked at him now, I noticed that it was starting to go gray on the left side—the silver hairs sparkled like stars nestled among the black.

Dad looked me up and down. "Is that a new outfit?"

"Yeah," I said brightly, pleased that he'd noticed. Glad I changed, I thought, giving myself a mental pat on the back.

Dad gave a little shrug. "Well, I guess that's what they're wearing these days," he said, almost to himself.

Suddenly, my mental pat felt more like a slap. What is that supposed to mean? I wondered. Dad made it sound like I looked horrible. And worse, like I just threw on whatever all the other kids did, like some kind of mindless amoeba. Not that amoebas wear clothes. But you know what I mean. "This is what *I'm* wearing," I said.

"Hey, Dad." Lionel trudged down the stairs with Mom right behind him.

I had to swallow a little giggle. Lionel was wearing a baseball cap.

"Hey, sport," Dad said, holding out his arms to Lionel.

Okay, here is another thing that drives me insane about Dad. Lionel is totally not a sport. *I'm* a sport. Lionel is lousy at games and looks like a Slinky in an earthquake when he runs. But, whatever. He's a guy, so he gets "sport."

"Hello, Howard," Mom said to Dad, who nodded at her and said, "Jane." Mom and Dad always act like people who work in the same office. It's really strange to think that they were ever married. I guess the only two things they really have in common are Lionel and me.

Dad hugged Lionel, then stepped back to look at him. "What's with the hat?" he asked, tugging on the bill of the Red Sox cap Lionel had on.

Lionel grinned. "What can I say? I love the Sox."

I was impressed with Lionel's cover story. Unfortunately, I knew it wasn't really going to fly with Dad.

"Well, you're not wearing it to dinner," Dad said in this kind-of-playing-but-really-not voice.

Lionel put his palm on top of his cap. "I wear it all the time. I like it."

"Not tonight," Dad said. His mouth was smiling, but his eyes were frowning as he yanked the cap off Lionel's head. "We're going to a restau—"

There was this horrible moment of silence as my father stared at Lionel's bald head. So that was the solution Mom had come up with—she'd just cut all of Lionel's hair as short as the chunk I'd taken out. There was still hair on Lionel's head, but it was very, very short, and so light it was almost invisible. Kind of like a peach.

In this weird way, I thought it looked kind of cool.

"Oh my . . ." Dad's eyes flashed to Mom. "You let him do this?" he demanded.

"It's just hair," Mom said. Her face was like stone. This is how she gets when Dad gets mad. She turns icy.

"It's *more* than hair, Jane," Dad snapped. "It's how the world sees him. He looks like one of those skinheads."

I opened my mouth to confess that Lionel's haircut was the result of my spazzitude, not a premeditated fashion statement, but my brother flashed me a *Don't say a word* look, then said, "Dad, I did it. Mom didn't even know about it."

Suddenly, I felt awful for Lionel. I knew how excited he'd been to see Dad, and now it was ruined. Thanks to me. And he'd just totally covered for me. Lionel hates lying, but I guess he figured that this was only a little flie. Besides, my brother must have known that if he told the real story, Dad would freak out at me for using the clippers, then at Lionel for letting me use them, then at Mom for letting us run wild.

Dad narrowed his eyes at Lionel, then looked at Mom again. "Don't you supervise them?"

I saw Mom inhale, and I knew that she was doing this yoga breath thing that she claims is very calming. Then she said, "This conversation is over, Howard. If you want to discuss Lionel's haircut, I suggest we talk another time." She gave Lionel a kiss on the cheek. "Have fun." Mom ran her hand playfully over his fuzzy scalp and smiled reassuringly. Then she looked over at me and winked.

I saw the muscles in Dad's jaw clench, but finally he let out this big whoosh of air, and turned to open the door. "I'll have them back before nine-thirty," Dad said in his professional office-worker voice.

"Bye, Mom," Lionel said. He sounded kind of sad.

"Bye." I glanced back at Mom as I followed Dad and Lionel out the door. Suddenly, I wasn't looking forward to this dinner very much. I love my dad, but he isn't any fun when he's angry.

I was in for a horrible night. And it was all my fault.

I looked out at our house from the backseat of Dad's rental car as we pulled up to the curb in front. For a minute, I felt as though I was seeing it through my dad's eyes—the shutter with the slat missing outside my window on the second floor, the grass that had grown over the edge of the side-walk, the scraggly miniature azalea bushes that never really bloomed. It wasn't a horrible house, but it was far from perfect. Still, I couldn't wait to get inside and curl up under my covers.

We had gone to our favorite restaurant, Tía Alma, where they have excellent Mexican food, and Dad tried to make up with Lionel by joking about his hair, but Lionel just sulked until Dad turned to me and asked about my science grade. I told him I'd brought it up, but I still got a lecture about how I'd never get into a good college if I didn't start working hard now. Then Dad told us all about the "family vacation" he'd planned with Marci and Daniel. Lionel hadn't said anything, but I could tell his feelings were hurt. I knew mine were. I mean, weren't Lionel and I family? Why weren't we invited? Anyway, I was feeling so stressed around Dad that I ate about five million chips dipped in Alma's special green sauce, and by the time my chile relleno showed up I thought I was going to barf. But Dad hates it when we "waste" food, so I forced myself to eat half of it and then took the rest home in a doggie bag. *Ugh*.

Now we were all sitting in the dark car without moving. No one spoke.

"So," Dad said brightly, then stopped. I guess he didn't know where to go from there.

"Thanks for taking us out, Dad," I told him.

"Yeah," Lionel added.

"I've missed you guys," Dad said. He looked from Lionel to me, then back again. "But I'll be back in town soon."

"I wish you could stay to see my soccer game tomorrow," I said.

"Me, too, sweetie. But I have to get back to work. You understand."

I nodded, but I didn't really understand. Lots of parents worked, but they managed to come to a soccer game now and then. Mom had come to four. Still, I knew there was no point in arguing. He wasn't coming. End of story.

Lionel leaned over, and Dad gave him a hug. I pecked Dad on the cheek, and Lionel and I stepped out of the car.

"I'll see you soon!" Dad promised. "And I'll talk to you even sooner."

"Love you," I said.

"Good. Me, too," Dad said, grinning, and I shut the door. Then Lionel and I stood there in silence as Dad drove away, the red taillights of his white rental fading into the darkness like embers from a fire.

I don't know why, but I always feel sadder when I see my dad than I do when I don't see him for a long time. I guess it reminds me that he isn't around, or something. I snuck a look at Lionel. By the expression on his face, I was pretty sure he was feeling the same way I was.

"Come on," Lionel said. He jerked his head toward our house and started up the front walk.

"Wait," I said.

Lionel turned to face me. "What?"

I heaved a deep breath. "I just wanted to say . . . thanks."

"What for?"

Lionel's face was only half visible in the light from the streetlamp halfway down our block. The shadows struck his cheekbones, and for a moment, I was shocked at how much he looked like Dad. "Just . . . for not telling Dad that I accidentally shaved your head."

Lionel rubbed his scalp for a minute, and then actually let out a chuckle. "Oh man," he said, half laughing. "I am so going to get it at school tomorrow."

"Can I . . . can I feel it?" I asked.

Lionel rolled his eyes, but he leaned forward, and I rubbed his scalp. The short, bristly hairs tickled my fingers. "Cool," I said warmly.

Lionel smiled.

"And it looks good, too," I added. "Don't worry about what anyone says."

"Yeah?" Lionel looked dubious.

"Really, I mean it," I said. "You look like a marine."

Lionel laughed, and we both turned toward the house. "Just don't go telling everyone that you're the reason my head is shaved. Then I'll really look like a nork."

That's what he said—*nork*. He used my word. Suddenly, I was really glad that I hadn't told Tam about Lionel's hair. It would have been all over the school by now. "I'll never tell," I promised. "Gigantic mutant blood-sucking trolls couldn't get it out of me."

Lionel paused at the front door and stared at me. "You're such a weirdo," he said, then pushed open the door.

Mom was sitting on the couch watching when we walked inside. She put the movie she'd been watching on mute, looked at her watch, and grinned. "Nine twenty-seven," she said, shaking her head. "Your dad sure is punctual. Did you have fun?"

Lionel shrugged. "It was okay, I guess. I've got some homework to do. I'll see you in the morning." He tramped up the stairs.

Mom looked at me, and I walked over and snuggled next to her. "Everything okay?"

"Yeah," I told her. "It's just kind of hard."

"I know." Mom wrapped her arm around me and gave me a squeeze. We just sat there like that for a few minutes, and after a while, I felt my breathing fall into the rhythm of Mom's. For some reason, it made me feel better.

"Let's talk about something fun," Mom said

after a minute. "Are you excited about the sports banquet this weekend?"

"Define *excited*."

Mom scooched backward to look at me. "You're not excited? I thought that you and Tam had been talking about it for weeks."

I sighed. "Yeah. But this guy kind of asked me to go with him."

"Really?" Mom was giving me this thrilled smile.

"It's not good."

"No? Why not? Is he a jerk?"

"No . . . he's . . ." How could I explain this? "He's just kind of a nerd."

"Oh," Mom said, nodding. "A cool nerd?"

I rolled my eyes. "I guess."

"Hmm. And you don't want to go with him."

"Well . . ." I hesitated. "He's okay, but . . ."

"You had someone else in mind?" Mom finished for me.

Freaky. Sometimes, I swear, Mom can read my thoughts. "Yeah," I admitted. "So what do I do?"

"Oh, gosh," Mom said with a laugh. "Don't ask me. I'm terrible at this stuff."

"Yeah, look at who *you* married." The words hung in the air for a moment before I clapped a hand over my mouth. I hadn't meant to say that! I'd never said anything *like* that before.

Mom looked surprised for a moment, then smiled at me sympathetically. "Your dad and I loved each other," Mom said, as she stroked my hair. "I know you don't remember, but we were happy for a long time."

I swallowed hard. It was just so hard to imagine that Mom and Dad had ever gotten along. "What happened?" I asked.

"I don't know, sweetheart." Mom continued to stroke my hair, but she had this faraway look on her face. "Sometimes people just grow apart. And it's really hard when that happens. You don't want to believe that someone you've been so close to could seem almost like a stranger."

An image of Tam flashed into my mind. "Yeah," I said quietly. "I guess I know what you mean."

Mom looked down at me and smiled. "But in the end, it all worked out. I got to do things I never would have been able to do if I'd stayed with your father. I built a business all by myself, and I learned how to be independent, and I made new friends. And those are good things."

I tried to imagine what I would get to do without Tam, but it wasn't easy. My life without her seemed kind of . . . blank.

Mom leaned over and kissed me on the forehead and whispered, "It gets easier."

I looked up at her and tried to smile, but it came out kind of weak. I hoped she was right.

"And as for your date," Mom added, "I can't tell you what to do."

Why not? I wanted to ask. Everyone else does. The TV glowed blue, casting eerie shadows on her face.

"Do you want a cookie?" Mom asked after a while. "I made chocolate-chip."

"No, thanks," I said. "I think I'll just head upstairs."

Mom touched my hair, tucked it behind my ear. "Okay. I'm here if you need me."

I gave her a hug, then headed up to my room.

---

squash \\'skwash\\   **1:** a feeling that your heart has been squeezed and leaves you all gooey inside **2:** the subject of extreme like

"Hey, Peebles. Hey, lazy cat." Peebles was curled up on my window seat. I went and sat beside her without turning on the light. I was surprised by how many stars I could see. The tree outside my window had lost a lot of leaves, and the little lights twinkled through bare branches. "Pretty," I said, stroking Peebles's fur. Peebles didn't bother waking up, just started purring in her sleep.

Sighing, I walked over to my desk and switched on the lamp. I was about to turn on the computer when I noticed the old LFC notebook sitting there. I had homework to do, but I just couldn't help myself. I flipped it open to the first page.

> First meeting of the LFC.
> President: Tamara
> Vice President: Renee
> Secretary: Allie
> Tamara's squashes: Bobby F.,
>   David S., David D., Franklin L.,
>   and Chris G.

Renee's squashes: Bill T., James
    R., George W., and David D.
Allie's squashes: Chris G. and
    Franklin L.

That's weird, I thought, looking over the page. I hadn't remembered that Tam had liked Chris in the beginning. Or that I had liked Franklin Linning. That was kind of funny, actually. Franklin had a big head—I mean, literally a big head in comparison to his tiny body—and he was super quiet. I guess he had nice eyes, though. I was pretty sure that I had never really liked him, but I felt like I had to have more than one crush in order to be in the club.

Sitting down, I thought back to the third grade, remembering when Tam had told me about her idea for the crush club. She had been all hot on the idea. But I wasn't. I didn't have any crushes.

"Don't be stupid," Tam had said. "Of course you do! What about Chris?"

"Who?" I asked.

"What do you mean, who? The cutest guy in school!" Tam cried.

I smiled at the memory. The next day, Tam had pointed out Chris during lunch, and I had to admit that he was cute. Way cute. So he was the first guy on my crush list.

I flipped through the notebook, scanning the "Squash Lists." Tam and Renee changed their crushes like they changed their underwear— there were new names added and old ones crossed off at every meeting. But mine stayed the same, except that after three weeks Franklin fell off the list, thanks to the famous incident in which he stuck his finger in the pencil sharpener. After that I thought he was kind of dumb. But Chris stayed—and he remained the only name on my list.

Tossing the notebook aside, I lay back on my bed and stared at the ceiling. It was bizarre to think that my major crush on Chris had basically started because I was looking for a name to put on my list. And then, I guess it just became a habit. But when I stopped to think about it, I couldn't really put my finger on just what it was that I liked about him. I mean, he was cute, sure. But so what?

I racked my brain, but I couldn't really think

of anything we'd ever said to each other—I mean, aside from that time he asked me for a pen. And all those times he hadn't gotten my jokes.

The thought actually made me laugh. Peebles let out a *browr* and looked up at me.

"Oh, go back to sleep," I told her. "Nothing important." Suddenly, I spotted my soccer notebook on my shelf. I pulled it down, and flipped it open to the first page, settling back down on my bed. "'One day till sixth grade, and Tam is afraid of looking like a nork,'" I read.

Well, she solved that problem, I thought. She just found Renee, and became a glommer.

It was funny to think about—I'd never thought of Tam as someone who worried about being a nerd. She had never thought about that stuff in elementary school. But now, she seemed to think about it all the time.

Peebles settled back down and I hauled myself off the bed and started to peel off my clothes. Forget homework, I decided. I was too tired for it, anyway. It was all I could do to change into my nightshirt and go through my usual tooth-brushing, face-washing thing. I skipped the floss.

Climbing into bed, I clicked off the lamp and stared out the window at the glimmering dark. I pulled my dark blue plaid sheets over my lips and breathed through my nose, thinking about the notebooks, and Tam. She was definitely changing . . . and I wasn't. I guess we were starting to grow apart, like Mom had said. I only had one question.

How in the world do you divorce your best friend?

- 12 -

frieend \ 'freend \ *n* : a fiend in friend's clothing

"So what's the plan?" Tam asked as she walked up to my locker. That was the first thing she said to me. Not *Hello*. Not *What's up?* No, it was all, "You've got to do this Orren thing *today*. People are starting to ask me if he's your boyfriend." Leaning back, she knocked her head against the lockers, like she was faced with some kind of enormous calamity.

Wondering who in the world besides Renee could have asked Tam if Orren was my boyfriend, I hauled my English book out of my locker and slipped it into my backpack. "Tam, did you tell Justin that I didn't want to go to the banquet with Orren?"

Embarrassment skittered across Tam's face, then disappeared. "Well, you don't."

"But I don't want Orren to know that." I slammed shut my locker and faced her. "Besides,

I hadn't even told you whether I wanted to go when you talked to Justin."

Tam rolled her eyes. "I knew that it wasn't even *possible* that you wanted to go with him."

"Look," I said, hitching my backpack higher on my shoulder, "I don't want to be Orren's date. But Orren is a nice guy, and I don't want to hurt his feelings, either."

"Which is why we need to come up with a plan," Tam shot back. "So that you can get this over with."

I was starting to feel like Tam was more of a frieend than a friend. She didn't care about Orren. And she didn't care about whether I liked Orren or not. She just wanted to get rid of him because he was embarrassing her in some way. I mean, it was kind of funny to think that Tam would be worried because some guy had asked me out. It didn't really have anything to do with her. But on the other hand, Tam lived in the real middle-school world, where people judged you by your friends. If she was friends with me and I was friends with Orren, Tam would be lower down on the middle-school food chain—closer to the Dweebosaurus. And once you're low on that chain, it's pretty easy to become extinct.

"What am I going to say to him?" I demanded. "I can't tell him that I'm going, just not with him."

"Why not?"

I gaped at her. "Because he's a *human being*!"

"Tell him you already have a date," Tam suggested.

"But that's a lie! And it'll be totally obvious when I show up without a date."

"Well . . . maybe you could ask someone else," Tam suggested.

"Like Chris," I whispered. Actually, this wasn't a bad idea. Orren already knew about my crush. He'd probably even understand. . . .

"Chris already has a date."

Momentarily lost in my fantasy about going to the banquet with Chris, sitting next to Chris, talking to Chris, it took almost a full minute for Tam's words to register. *"What?"*

"Renee asked him yesterday." Tam's face had turned pink, and she looked kind of guilty. "I thought you knew."

"But she knows I like him—"

"Allie, *everybody* likes him," Tam shot back. "He's the hottest guy in the entire school. It's not like you can just call dibs on him, or something."

I stared at her. I couldn't believe she had just said that. She knew that I'd liked Chris for *years*. Renee knew it, too. And, even if Renee wasn't my friend, Tam was. Or she was supposed to be. Why hadn't she warned me that Renee was into him?

"Look, just tell Orren that you're going to the banquet with the girls' soccer team," Tam suggested. "He won't want to be the only guy at the table."

Actually, I wasn't so sure that Orren would really care, but I just nodded. I didn't trust myself to speak. I could feel hot tears pooling in my eyes, and I knew that a single word would send them spilling down my face. I couldn't believe that Renee had asked Chris to the banquet after she made me feel like an idiot for liking him. I couldn't believe that Renee would stab me in the back like that. Or that Tam would act like it was no big deal. Like this thing with Orren was a problem that needed to be solved right away, but my feelings . . . well, who cared?

"So wait a minute, Tam," I said slowly, as things began to click together in my brain. "You're so eager for me to ditch Orren, but who are you going with? Do you even have a date to the banquet?"

Tam's face turned pale, and the muscles in her jaw tensed. "I'm going with Tom."

"Tom Fine?" I repeated. Chris's best friend. So she and Renee had planned it together. . . .

"Allie, are you listening to me?" Tam asked. "You have to do this today. It doesn't matter what you tell him. Just get rid of him."

I nodded again. *So, Orren, the girls on the soccer team are all planning to sit together*, I rehearsed mentally. But this speech was all wrong. For one thing, it wasn't true. But beyond that, I'd sort of thought I'd be sitting with Tam at the sports banquet. I mean, that had been our plan since the first week of school. Come to think of it, though, Tam hadn't really mentioned it lately. But if she wasn't planning on sitting with me, why would she care whether Orren was my date or not? Then again,

Tam would probably want to sit with Renee, and I wasn't sure that I really wanted to sit with her and Chris when they were on a kind of date-type thing.

"Tam . . ." My voice was thick, but I forced out the words. "Are we sitting together at the banquet?"

Tam let out her breath in this big whoosh. "Look, Renee absolutely will not sit with Orren. So if you want to sit with us . . ."

Her unfinished sentence hung in the air, a silent threat.

So she had made her choice. If I wanted to be her friend, I had to follow the rules.

The bell rang, and Tam touched me on the shoulder. "Good luck. Let me know how it goes." Like I was taking an algebra quiz.

Kids started to stream toward their homerooms, like ants pouring from a crushed anthill, as Tam turned away. I saw Justin at his locker at the end of the hall and I thought about what he'd said the day before. That most girls would have said no to Orren without thinking about it. But it was too late—I'd already thought about it. And once you thought about things, you had to do what was right. "No," I whispered.

Tam froze in her steps, then turned back toward me slowly. "What?"

I shook my head. "No," I whispered. I cleared my throat.

"What do you mean, no?"

"I mean"—I took a deep breath—"I think I'll just go to the banquet with Orren. Thanks," I added, because I felt like I needed to say something.

"What—what do you mean?" Tam's eyes reminded me of closed doors. "You're choosing Orren over me?"

I shook my head. You're the one who's made the choice, I thought, but that wasn't what I said. "No. I just don't want to ditch him. He's a nice guy, Tam. I can't do it."

"Fine. Have it your way," Tam snapped. Then she stormed away.

"This isn't my way," I said, but it was too late. She was too far away. She couldn't hear a word I said.

———◆———

streep•er \'streep-er \ *n* : someone who plays both offense and defense on a soccer team

"This is it," Jack said as she slung her arm around my shoulders, "last game of the year."

"I can't believe the season is over," Elena said as she yanked on her cleats. "I feel like we just got into the swing of things."

"Not yet," Sarah pointed out in her shy voice, her dark eyes serious. "We've still got an hour and a half left."

"I can't believe we have to play Saint Agnes again," Sally said as she gathered her long cornrows into a scrunchie.

"Those girls had better be ready to get their little buttery yellow uniforms dirty," Jack said.

I shifted uncomfortably on the splintery bench. Most of the ancient green paint was worn away, and the old wood dug through the seat of my uniform—but mostly I was antsy because I was eager to play. It was a crisp fall day—only a few cottonball clouds floating overhead in a sea of blinding blue.

A perfect day for kicking butt.

"Go, team, go!" Justin's voice shouted behind me. Turning, I saw Justin and Chris headed toward our bench. I glanced at Chris, then looked away. Seeing him was kind of strange. It left me feeling sort of hollow, and sad. But not sad because I felt like my heart was broken. Sad because I felt like something had shifted. His blue eyes didn't fill me with familiar fluttery excitement. I didn't feel his presence like a warm blanket wrapped around me.

After three years, I had discovered that I didn't really care about him anymore. Just like that. Not that it made what Renee had done any less heinous.

"So, is everybody going to the banquet tomorrow?" Jack asked, holding up a packet of tickets. "Anyone need to buy a ticket?"

"I bought mine two weeks ago," Elena said. "I've already got my dress."

"Me, too," Justin joked. "How do the tickets work? Can we all sit together?"

"First come, first seated," Jack explained.

"Allie, if we get there first, we'll save you and Orren seats," Jack said. She, Elena, Sally, Justin, and two other guys from the soccer team were all going together. "And you should do the same, just in case Justin takes forever to get ready."

"Oh, please," Chris said with a groan, "you're always late."

"That is such a lie!" Jack screeched.

I smiled, but my head was spinning. Jack was going to save seats for me and Orren. Like it was no big deal. And no one had protested.

"Okay, well, we've got to get to our game," Justin said. "See you after. Good luck!"

"Right back at you," I told him.

Justin gave me a huge smile, revealing a crooked tooth—the one right between his canine and the big one in the front. His smile was really cute, I thought as he trotted off with Chris.

Funny how I had never noticed that before.

An hour later, I was in the game, and there was nothing but the ball. It was as though the world had ceased to exist, as though I had ceased to exist. There was no team. There was no Cleveland Middle School. No Saint Agnes. No Tam. No Orren. No Renee or Chris. Only a ball and a goal. . . .

Slam!

With a sliding kick, I knocked the ball away from the Saint Agnes right wing, shooting beneath her leg. Like lightning, Sally leaped in and slapped the ball toward their goal. I didn't even realize that I had gotten up, that I was chasing her, until I was closer to the goal than she was.

The whole game had been this way—back and forth with Saint Agnes. We were down by one, but those parolies were starting to get tired. I could feel it. And I was just getting warmed up.

A quick pass to Jack, who slammed it toward me. In an instant, I headed the ball toward their goal. Score!

We were tied. Two minutes later, Elena stole the ball and darted back toward Saint Agnes's territory. She was about to take a shot when one of the Saint Agnes girls dug her in the shin wth her cleat. Elena fell to her knees, and the ref called the foul. I looked to the sidelines . . . just as I'd feared, Coach was motioning to me to kick. This was my shot. My chance to win the game.

For a moment, I was struck with the strangeness of it—it was my chance to prove Coach

Connors right—or wrong. She said I had the talent. She believed in my scoring. But I knew how to defend, that was my thing.

Then again, I thought, maybe my thing isn't my only thing anymore. Maybe I wasn't just a striker or a sweeper. Maybe I was a streeper: both at once.

One step. Two steps. I ran toward the ball. It was like I had super vision. I could see every crack, every stain, every pore in the surface of the ball. Like it was as big as the earth . . . Don't miss, I thought as my leg swung toward the ball.

And I didn't.

A moment later, the whistle blew—game over.

I just stood there, breathing hard until Jack ran up behind me and pounced.

"We did it!" Elena screamed.

For a moment, I felt like I was floating . . . and then I realized that I really was floating, that my teammates had picked me up and were carrying me off the field.

"Put me down!" I shouted. I was worried that they might drop me. "Put me down!" But no one heard me. They were singing and laughing too loudly to hear.

I could see out over all of the green practice fields from up there. The golden and orange leaves were racing across the grass. I felt the sun beat down on my face, and the wind blow my damp hair back.

I remembered how Tam had wanted me to join the cheer squad. And maybe, I thought, if I had, she and Renee and I would still be friends. But this wouldn't have happened. I never would have had this moment.

Suddenly, my life without Tam was starting to seem a lot less blank.

sulk•a•bra•tion \'sulk-a-bray-shen\ *n* : the worst party in the history of partydom, one that promises nothing but humiliation, bad dancing, and rubbery grilled chicken

"What are you all dressed up for?" Lionel asked as I walked down the stairs in my never-before-worn-in-public long black skirt and hot-pink blouse, along with my chunky shoes. It was Saturday evening. D-Day. Dork Day.

"I'm going to the sports banquet," I told him. "Some of us actually get off the couch and run around once in a while." So what if I was going to a major sulkabration? I wasn't about to admit that to Lionel.

Lionel flipped the channel to MTV. "You got all dressed up for your date with Bore-en? It'll probably be the thrill of his life."

God, I was still not used to being the grist of the gossip mill. "How do you know about Orren? You don't even know who he is!"

Lionel rolled his eyeballs back into his head. "He rides our bus, moron."

"Oh, right." I'd actually kind of forgotten that Orren rode our bus. He still always sat in the front, and he got on at the last stop. I was usually too busy chatting with Justin or finishing homework to pay much attention to him. Wow, I thought. It's actually kind of odd that I had never asked him to join us.

"I can't believe you're going out with that guy. He's the biggest nerd at Cleveland."

"Counting you?" I snapped.

"Counting Shaffer Spence, winner of the regional science fair, counting Victoria Lakes, whose glasses are so thick they could be used to start a fire, counting Jeffrey Jackson, whose face looks like it's about to erupt," Lionel said, ticking off every major nerd in our school on his fingers, "counting *everyone*."

"Look, it's not like Orren is my boyfriend. We're just—" I hesitated. What were we? Orren was just my lab partner and a nice person whose feelings I didn't want to hurt—but that didn't sound very good, so I went with,

"We're just friends. And I'm not going to treat him like dirt just because everyone thinks he's a dweeb. I mean, so what if he's nerdy? At least he's different."

"'Different' is an understatement." Lionel snorted. He looked at me for a minute, and I thought I saw his expression soften. "You're just like Mom."

I was just about to ask Lionel what in the world he meant by that, when Mom breezed in, jingling her car keys. "Ready, Allie?" She smiled at me. "You look beautiful."

I blushed. *Beautiful* isn't a word I get a lot. I guess I tend to think of myself as borderline pretty at best. But it felt good to hear.

"Do you want to come along, Lionel?" Mom asked. "I have to drop Allie at the banquet."

Lionel shook his head and turned back to the TV. "Jed is coming over later. We're going to network his laptop and my computer and play some online video games."

I rolled my eyes. And my brother was calling Orren a nerd? "Have fun," I chirped as I followed Mom out the door.

"You, too," Lionel called sarcastically. "Tell Orren I said hi."

Even the norks were mocking me now.

I couldn't wait to get this evening over with.

"Is that him?" Mom whispered a few moments later as we pulled up to the rear entrance to the cafetorium. Orren was standing alone outside the double doors. He was wearing a new-looking green shirt and a funky blue-and-maroon tie with a pair of black pants.

"Yeah."

"He's cute," Mom said brightly. "When you said 'nerd,' I was thinking of Lionel's friends."

I laughed, wishing that I had a tape recorder. "Well, he doesn't usually look this good," I admitted. Actually, with the funky tie, Orren's frizzed-out hair actually looked borderline cool. And the green of his shirt brought out the color of his eyes.

"Have fun," Mom said. Leaning over, she gave me a peck on the cheek. "Knock 'em dead."

I gave her a wavery smile and took a deep breath. "I'll see you at ten."

"Hey!" Orren said as I stepped out of the car. "You're three minutes late." He grinned, though, so I knew he was kidding.

"You look great," I told him.

Orren looked like I'd just handed him a check for a million dollars. "Yeah?"

I laughed. "Yeah."

He stood there awkwardly for a moment, so I cleared my throat and gestured toward myself. "Oh! You look great, too," Orren said quickly.

"Nice job," I told him.

"You want to go inside?"

Not really, I said mentally, but what I said out loud was, "Sure."

There was a burst of music as we walked into the banquet. I was surprised to see that the center had been cleared to make a dance floor, and there was a DJ playing music. I hadn't expected that.

"Allie! Orren! Over here!" Jack was going Muppet at us like crazy. Elena was next to her, and she waved, too.

I took a step toward my friends and froze in my tracks. Tam and Renee were at a table ten feet away. I was going to have to walk right past Tam.

Renee was leaning toward Chris, whispering something in his ear. Tam glanced at them, then looked down at the table, obviously bored. Tom wasn't saying anything. I took the opportunity to walk past her, staring in the opposite direction, as if the blank wall at the end of the cafetorium was the most fascinating thing in the world. I made it past her without making eye contact, and breathed a sigh of relief as I reached Jack's table.

"Isn't this great?" Elena asked as we sat down. "I love the glitter on the tables."

I looked around. Actually, considering that we were sitting in the cafetorium, the place did look pretty elegant. The tables had been spread with white tablecloths and covered in colorful glitter. The centerpieces were gerber daisies in Crayola shades, and the ceiling was filled with helium balloons in blue and red, our school colors.

"I love the DJ," Jack said as she bopped along to the beat.

"Is this where all of the cool cats are sitting?" Justin asked as he appeared behind Elena's chair.

"Yeah, but we'll let you sit with us, anyway," Jack told him.

"Hey, man, what's up?" Justin asked as he slid into the chair next to Orren and gave him a high five. "Lookin' sharp."

"Yeah, I love that tie," Jack said warmly.

Orren touched his tie self-consciously and said, "Thanks."

I tried to keep my mind on the conversation around me, but I was too distracted by the fact that we were sitting so close to Tam. I wondered whether she was having a good time. It hadn't really looked like it when I walked in. Good, I thought meanly. It serves her right. But there was still a part of me that felt bad. I didn't want Tam to be miserable—I wanted both of us to be happy.

The DJ put on a bouncy dance beat, and Elena grinned. "I feel like dancing," she said. "Who's with me?"

"I'm in," Jack said.

"Me, too," Sally said, standing up.

"Me, three," Justin agreed.

"Let's go," Sally said, pulling Evan and Sam—Justin's soccer friends—out of their chairs by the hands. "I can't wait to shake my booty."

"Anyone else?" Evan asked. "Orren—you can't leave me alone out there, man."

I glanced at Orren. He had this look on his face—I don't know, like Evan was an ax-wielding maniac, or something. "I'm guessing you're not a big dancer," I said to Orren.

"Not really," he admitted. "But you go."

"You're going to sit here by yourself?" I asked him.

"I don't mind." I knew it was probably true, but still. I minded.

"You guys go ahead," I told my friends, secretly relieved. I really didn't want the whole school to see me dancing with Orren.

"You sure?" Jack asked. "Come on, Orren. It'll be fun."

"Just this one song," Elena begged.

"No, no really—" I started, but Orren cut me off.

"Okay," he said, sliding back his chair. He must have seen the horror on my face, because his eyebrows drew together in confusion. "You want to, right?"

Elena clapped eagerly, so I nodded. She grabbed our hands and dragged us to the dance floor. Jack and Justin let out a whoop as we formed a circle. Justin launched into some weird version of the funky chicken, and Jack was managing to dance without actually moving her feet. She was a total arm dancer. Elena bopped around all over the place, like some kind of Mexican jumping bean.

We were the only ones dancing, and I felt pretty conspicuous as I tried to dance and appear invisible at the same time. But that only lasted a minute. It was almost as though everyone had just been waiting for someone to start the dancing, because after about two minutes, Sarah bopped out to join us. Then half of the field hockey team headed toward the dance floor, followed by a couple of cheer squadders. Everyone was dancing in big circles of friends—except the footballers, who mostly lurked in the corner trying to look cool. The DJ turned up the volume.

Orren did the step-together-step-back that most guys do, but he wasn't bad. He actually smiled at me and leaned over to whisper in my ear. "I've been practicing," he admitted, which made me laugh. Orren laughed, too. I looked out at the other dancers, expecting to see Tam. She's an excellent dancer, and loves music. But she wasn't there. A moment later, I spotted her still sitting at her table. Her eyes flicked to me for a moment.

Without even realizing what I was doing, I gestured to her to come over. "Come dance," I whispered, even though I knew she couldn't hear me.

Tam looked surprised . . . but a moment later, her eyes flicked to Renee. And even though Renee had her back turned toward Tam, Tam still didn't get up. She looked at me and shook her head slightly, then looked down at the table.

Orren caught the look. "What's wrong?" he asked, leaning toward me. "Tam doesn't want to dance?"

"Tam doesn't know what she wants," I told him. Suddenly, I didn't feel much like dancing anymore. "Do you want to get out of here?" I asked, pointing to the exit sign.

Orren nodded. "Yeah." He looked relieved.

Elena grabbed my hand as we started to walk off. "Back in a minute," I told her. I waved to Jack and Justin, who frowned slightly.

The night was surprisingly quiet as the cafetorium door closed behind us. The air was mild—it was Indian Summer—with only a slight chill as we walked away from the school, toward the soccer fields.

Looking up at the sky, I spotted a brilliant star. "Star light, star bright," I said, half to myself. "Make a wish." I closed my eyes. The ache in my heart told me to wish that Tamara and I could be best friends again, but I wasn't even sure that was what I wanted anymore. Then I thought about Chris. My reflex wish for three years had been to wish that he would like me. But I didn't really care about that, either. In the end, I decided that I didn't know what to wish for. So I just gave up and wished for world peace. That's always a safe one.

When I opened my eyes, Orren was looking at me. "What did you wish for?" he asked.

"If I tell you, it won't come true."

A corner of Orren's mouth drifted up. "It

won't come true, anyway. You just wished on Venus."

"What?" I stared at the sky, where my wishing star glittered. "How do you know?"

"Venus is the brightest thing in the sky," Orren said, staring at the darkness above us. "It's practically all you can see when you live in the city. The light from all of the buildings hides most of the stars. But look, you can still see a few. That's Cygnus, the swan. It has a star with a planet in orbit around it."

I looked to where he was pointing, suddenly feeling very small beneath the enormous universe. It made me feel as though there was nothing I could do that would matter very much. In a way, it was frightening. But it was comforting, too. Because I knew that there wasn't a mistake I could make that would disturb the universe. It was funny how I only ever thought about stuff like that when I was with Orren. "How do you know so much about the stars?"

He shrugged. "I don't know. Books. TV. Stars are interesting." He turned his face back to the sky, and his expression held a mixture of wonder and happiness . . . and some of that feeling rubbed off on me. Orren was right—the stars *were* interesting. And beautiful.

I looked at him, watching him watch the sky, and my heart gave a sudden lurch. No, no—don't get me wrong. It wasn't love, or even extreme like, or any of that romantic junk. Ew—*no way*. No, the feeling was more like . . . like affection, or something. Like the way I felt about Peebles. And, for the first time, I realized I was having fun.

For some reason, I thought about what Lionel had said to me earlier. That I was just like Mom. Actually, I thought that Orren was more like Mom than I was. They both did their own thing and didn't care about what other people thought. I wished I were like that. The truth was, though, I *did* care.

Orren looked at me, blinking, like he was just waking up from a dream. "We're probably missing the dinner. Maybe we should head back."

I wasn't hungry, and I didn't really want to go back inside. I felt like everyone was looking at me there, forming opinions and judgments. It made it hard to think. Out here, alone with Orren, I could breathe. "Do you want to?"

"Not yet."

"Me, neither." Orren turned back to face the stars.

We stood out there for a few more minutes, until I started to feel cold. Orren gave me his jacket, and then we headed back to the banquet.

The loud music washed over me as I stepped into the cafetorium. It took a moment for my eyes to adjust to the flashing lights, and I blinked as I felt someone squeeze me on the shoulder. I looked over into the warm dark eyes of Coach Connors.

"Allie," Coach said, "I'm glad you're here. I was worried when I didn't see you."

"I couldn't miss the banquet, Coach," I said with a smile.

Coach nodded, smiling. "You played well today." She was wearing a pink slip dress that skimmed lightly over her muscles. I was sort of surprised by her dress—I had never suspected

Coach Connors could own anything so girly. But then I remembered my own pink shirt. I guess we're all more complicated than we seem. "You did what I've been expecting you to do all year," she added.

I looked over at Orren, who grinned. "I guess maybe I am a striker after all," I said to the coach. Maybe I was better at taking risks than I thought.

"I always knew you could do it," Coach said. "You were the one who needed to learn that you could." She patted me on the arm. "Will I see you on the indoor soccer team next semester?"

"I hadn't really thought about it—"

"I'll take that as a yes," Coach said. "We need you." She nodded to Orren, then gave me a smile—a huge smile. I smiled back. Then she walked away.

"She's kind of scary," Orren whispered once Coach Connors was out of earshot.

"Nah," I told him as I watched the coach stride across the room. "She's just fearless. And she expects everyone else to be, too." As I watched her glide across the room, her posture perfect, I realized that Coach's confidence gave her a certain kind of freedom. Coach was almost like a bird—a hawk, or an eagle, maybe—who doesn't have to worry too much about what the world thinks, because she flies above it.

"Coach Condor," I whispered, smiling.

"What?" Orren asked.

I flushed a little, shaking my head. "Oh, nothing. I was just thinking that Coach Connors is like a condor."

Orren nodded, his face thoughtful. "You know," he said as we moved toward our table, "condors are interesting birds. They feed on dead animals. But they can attack live ones, too—they've been known to bring down deer."

I stopped in my tracks and blinked at him. Leave it to Orren to mess up my metaphor.

"Okay," I said finally, "she's not like a condor."

"They're huge," Orren went on, as though he hadn't heard me. "They have a nine- or ten-foot wingspan. They're pretty amazing in the air. And they're very rare."

I lifted my eyebrows at him. Ten-foot

wingspan? They must really soar. "So—she's kind of like a condor."

Orren snorted at me, like I was really hopeless. "It's a simile, Allie," he huffed. "You don't have to be so literal all the time."

non•shock•er \ non-'shok-er \: *n* : a surprise that, when you think about it, isn't really such a surprise, after all

I squeezed my history book between my belly and the edge of the lockers, flipping through the pages. I always do my homework on a piece of three-ring paper, then fold the page into my textbook. It's a horrible habit. First of all, it virtually guarantees that my locker will be a mess, because half the time the papers slip out of the books and fall to the bottom, like a pile of wet leaves beneath the bleachers. And for another thing, it always takes me forever to find my homework.

It's a strange addiction.

Finally, *finally*, after flipping through chapter seven about twelve times, my homework appeared on page 97. I picked it out and shoved it into the flap of my binder, then slammed my locker closed and turned toward class.

And there they were. Tam and Renee.

My feet did this bizarre kind of jerky robot dance as the sight of them stopped me in my tracks. For a moment, I considered turning around, heading the other way. I'd be late to class, my mind flashed, but it would be worth it.

But in the next moment, my body decided to move forward. Renee gave me this evil grin, but Tam gave me this look like, *Please don't*. I can't explain it, but those were the words stamped across her face: PLEASE DON'T.

I don't know what she thought I was going to do.

"Hi, Allie!" Renee said brightly as she walked up to me. She was wearing this matchy-matchy little blue sweater-and-miniskirt combo. How does she sit down in that thing? I wondered, eyeing the skirt.

"Hi, Renee." I didn't bother giving my face muscles a smile workout. I knew that Renee wouldn't be giving me the big hello unless she wanted to say something nasty, but I walked right into it.

"So—did you have fun at the banquet on

Saturday?" Renee asked. "You and your boyfriend looked like you were having a good time!"

I gritted my teeth. God, Renee was annoying. I looked at Tam, but she looked away. So she still wasn't going to stand up to Renee. I don't know why I was surprised. "We had a great time, thanks," I said, not even bothering to deny that Orren was my boyfriend. I knew she'd just said that to irk me. "Too bad your date looked miserable."

Tam gaped and Renee glared, but there wasn't really much that either one of them could say. Renee turned quickly on her heel and stalked off.

But Tam's dark eyes were locked on me. She didn't move.

It took Renee a minute to realize that Tam wasn't trotting after her. A worry line formed between her eyebrows. "Tam," she called. "Come on!"

Tam's eyes flicked to Renee, then back to me.

"I'm really glad you had a good time, Allie," Tam said quietly.

Don't follow her, I thought. You don't have to. But Tam was already in motion, hurrying after Renee.

Renee flashed me a triumphant smile, and a moment later, their retreating figures disappeared into the swirl of students racing to their second-period classes.

A cold hand of fear gripped my stomach and squeezed. This wasn't supposed to happen.

"Hey, are you okay?" asked a voice next to my ear. I looked up to see Justin standing there, peering at me. "You look kind of . . ." He shook his head. "I don't know."

"You're Justin Thyme," I said, sighing. "As usual."

Justin nodded, but he didn't ask questions. "You going my way?" he asked giving his chin a little jut toward the end of the hall.

"Sure am." We fell into step.

"So—Saturday was pretty fun," Justin said, giving me this sideways look.

"Oh, yeah," I agreed, trying to sound cheerful. "You were right—I'm really glad I went with Orren."

Justin cleared his throat. "So, uh, are you and Orren, like—boyfriend and girlfriend now?"

My eyes locked onto his face, trying to read his expression. Was Justin going to give me a hard time, now? I couldn't believe this. "We're *friends*."

"Oh." Justin nodded, looking relieved. "That's good."

"What's *that* supposed to mean?" I snapped. "Look, Orren is a really nice guy, and any girl would be lucky to go out with him. I am so sick of people putting him down because he's slightly strange. All right! So he's weird! So he's interested in typhoons, and algae, and looking at the stars. Is that such a crime? No! And I swear, if one more person tells me that he's a dork, I think I'm going to *lose it*! He's my friend! Okay? My *friend*!"

Justin's eyes were wide. "Uh . . . okay," he said uncertainly. "I just meant that it was, you know, good for *me*."

I stared at Justin for a moment as my heart did this slowing-down, speeding-up thing. But I didn't have time to wonder whether I was having a heart attack, because I was too busy trying to figure out what Justin meant. Good for *him*? Did he mean . . . ?

"So, uh, I'll see you at lunch?" Justin asked.

I nodded, unable to speak. Are you saying that you like me? I thought. My lips trembled, and I was about to ask, but I was too slow. Justin had already walked through Mrs. Pearson's classroom door, and the moment had passed.

Oh my God, I thought. The sudden realization stopped me in my tracks. It was like I had stuck my finger into a wall socket, or something—like my body was filled with electricity. Oh my God, I like Justin!

All this time, I'd been too busy paying attention to my crush on Chris to even notice Justin! But we had tons in common. We had a great time together. And he is funny, and sweet, and cute. . . . Of course I was crushing on him. He was more than a squash. He was real. When I thought about it, it was a complete nonshocker.

"Hey, Allie, hurry up!" Jack called as she jogged up to me. "We're going to be late to class!"

She poked me in the arm and we fell into a trot together.

"Lunch patio or cafetorium?" Jack asked. Translation: where should I find you at lunch?

"Lunch patio," I told her.

Jack nodded. "Save for a save." Translation: If you get there first, reserve my seat, and I'll do the same for you.

"And save a seat for Justin."

Jack rolled her eyes. "Thanks, Captain Obvious. Whoever gets there first saves five more."

"Don't you mean four more?"

Jack ticked off the names on her fingers. "You, me, Sally, Justin, Elena, and Orren," Jack explained. Like we ate lunch with Orren every day.

I spotted Orren at the end of the hall. He was reading a book and walking at the same time, headed toward our English class. I shook my head and smiled. The book was a biography of Benjamin Franklin. Where does he find these things? I wondered. "Cool," I told Jack. "See you then."

"See you!" Jack waved and trotted on as Orren disappeared into our classroom.

I hitched my backpack higher onto my back and took a step toward English.

Well, I thought as I headed to class, no matter how bad this day gets, at least I get to have lunch with my friends. Maybe we aren't the coolest kids at Cleveland. But what's the point of being cool when you never get to do what you want?

Suddenly, I realized something. I wasn't a Dweebosaurus, after all. I wasn't about to become extinct, and neither were my friends. If anyone was becoming extinct, it was Tam— the new glommer. She was disappearing, clinging onto Renee while I was learning how to do what I wanted. Like Mom. And Coach Connors. And Jack. And Orren.

Orren once told me that the dinosaurs eventually evolved into birds. Can you imagine that— a freaky giant lizard turning into a tiny chirping creature with feathers and the power to fly? But it just goes to show how much things can change when they have to adapt to a new environment.

That's kind of what happened to me, I guess. I went from feeling like a Dweebosaurus to becoming my own, new creature. Maybe one day, like Coach Condor, I'd learn to fly.

But, for now, I was happy just to be Allie Kimball. My own me. Unique, but not alone.

No. Not alone at all.

Lisa Papademetriou

has written and/or adapted more than thirty books for children and young adults, including titles in the Betty and Veronica, Lizzie McGuire, and That's So Raven book series. Lisa lives in Northampton, Massachusetts, with her husband, where she enjoys knitting, dancing around the house to eighties music, giving workshops on writing, playing the guitar (badly), and drinking large amounts of coffee.

To find out more about Lisa, visit www.lisapapa.com.